Famous photographer Quentin Berg stood up and rewound the film. "That's a wrap," he said.

"I am going directly to a spa at a location I have no intention of disclosing," Simone announced. "No one should even *try* to track me down, since I will be totally out of reach." Then she stomped out.

Jessica's ears perked up at Simone's words. With Simone out of the way, she might finally get a shot at modeling herself.

"If anyone needs me, I'm in the darkroom," Quentin said.

Jessica watched Quentin walk away, and a devious idea popped into her head. She waited until he had disappeared into the darkroom, then she looked around surreptitiously. Everybody around her was busy.

Her heart pounding in her chest, Jessica walked nonchalantly toward the camera. Then she clicked open the back of it, exposing the film. Holding her breath, she quickly shut it again. She glanced around the room quickly and let out her breath in a rush. Nobody had even noticed.

Jessica rubbed her hands together, unable to believe her luck. If everything went according to plan, she was on her way to stardom.

MODEL
FLIRT

Written by
Kate William

Created by
FRANCINE PASCAL

BANTAM BOOKS
NEW YORK • TORONTO • LONDON • SYDNEY • AUCKLAND

RL 6, age 12 and up

MODEL FLIRT

A Bantam Book / April 1997

Sweet Valley High® is a registered trademark of Francine Pascal.
Conceived by Francine Pascal.
Produced by Daniel Weiss Associates, Inc.
33 West 17th Street
New York, NY 10011.
Cover photography by Michael Segal.

ISBN: 0-553-57064-1

Published simultaneously in the United States and Canada

Bantam Books are published by Bantam Books, a division of Bantam
Doubleday Dell Publishing Group, Inc. Its trademark, consisting of the
words "Bantam Books" and the portrayal of a rooster, is Registered in U.S.
Patent and Trademark Office and in other countries. Marca Registrada.
Bantam Books, 1540 Broadway, New York, New York 10036.

PRINTED IN THE UNITED STATES OF AMERICA

OPM   0 9 8 7 6 5 4 3 2 1

To Hilary Bloom

Chapter 1

Sixteen-year-old Elizabeth Wakefield ducked into the darkroom of the art department at *Flair* magazine on Thursday afternoon, her whole body trembling in shock. She leaned against the heavy door of the outer chamber and wrapped her arms around her sides, squeezing her eyes shut. But there was no escaping the horrendous image that reappeared in her mind, clear as a summer day. The image was of her longtime boyfriend, Todd Wilkins, locked in a passionate embrace with Simone, a striking supermodel.

In the cool darkness of the closetlike space, Elizabeth replayed the scene she'd just witnessed like a movie in slow motion.

Opening credits. Elizabeth Wakefield is searching for her boyfriend, Todd Wilkins, to tell him that she misses him and that she is sorry they have spent so little time together this week. She pushes open the door of the main photography studio on the ninth floor. The room is shrouded in darkness. Todd, are you still here? she wonders. She flicks on the overhead light.

Tight close-up. Elizabeth stares in horror at the sight before her.

Simone's long arms are entwined around Todd's neck, her barely clothed body inches from his. Todd's hands are resting lightly on Simone's narrow hips. And his lips are closed on hers. Focus on Simone's smooth profile. And the angular cut of her sleek black hair. And the shiny gleam of her gold bikini.

Elizabeth gasps and stumbles backward, grabbing on to a table edge for support. Todd and Simone both turn at the sound. The blood rushes from Todd's face. Simone looks on coolly, triumphant sparks shooting from her ice blue eyes. A small smile curls on her artificially full red lips.

Elizabeth turns and flees. The End.

Elizabeth slid down the wall to the floor, her heart constricting in pain. *That's not the way it would have happened in a film,* she thought. In the movies, there were always happy endings. But not in real life. Real life was just betrayal and deception. A hot tear rolled down her cheek.

When Elizabeth and her twin sister, Jessica, had landed their positions as interns at *Flair* magazine, Elizabeth had thought a whole new world was opening up to her. But now she felt as though she were trapped on a uncharted desert island—*all alone*. Elizabeth leaned her head back against the door and closed her eyes, tasting the bittersweet saltiness of her tears.

She jolted at the sound of a door slamming shut.

"Elizabeth, where are you?" Todd called down the hallway.

Elizabeth stood up quickly and opened the interior door. She never wanted to see Todd again. And she particularly didn't think she could face him now. She crept into the developing room. A dim, red safelight cast an eerie glow in the otherwise dark room, and tall tubes that smelled of chemicals lined a long table. A row of prints hung from what looked like a clothesline, and Elizabeth stooped underneath it, looking for a way out.

Elizabeth caught sight of a side entrance and silently pushed it open. She looked around quickly, blinking in the light as she tried to orient herself. She was in some kind of prop room. A jumble of ladders and lights crowded the small space.

After weaving through the ladders, Elizabeth pulled open a door and found herself in a small photo studio. She breathed a sigh of relief, feeling safe in the hidden space.

But then she heard the sound of approaching footsteps.

"Elizabeth, wait!" Todd exclaimed, opening the door behind her.

At the sound of his voice, Elizabeth rushed across the room, hurrying through the swinging doors back into the main studio. She dodged some props and sprinted across the cavernous room. But Todd caught up with her at the door, grabbing her arm roughly.

Elizabeth shook off his hand. *"Don't touch me,"* she hissed through clenched teeth. "Don't *ever* touch me again."

"Fine!" Todd responded defensively, pulling his arm back.

"Sharing isn't my style," Elizabeth bit out angrily. "What's wrong? Isn't Simone woman enough for you?"

Todd's coffee brown eyes clouded over in pain. "Please, Elizabeth, let me explain," he pleaded.

For a moment Elizabeth softened. Todd's handsome face was so woeful that she had a sudden urge to hug him.

But then she remembered the horrible picture of Todd and Simone together, and a frozen calm fell over her. *It's too late,* she realized. Nothing that Todd said could take back what he had done. Nothing could erase the painful image engraved in her mind. "There's nothing to explain," Elizabeth said softly. "It's simple. You're not the person I thought you were." Then she shrugged. "I can do better."

Sparks of anger replaced the pain in Todd's eyes. He looked at her coldly, his face an implacable mask. "I guess I already have," he retorted.

Elizabeth winced at his cruel words. "I guess so," she responded sadly. "Good-bye, Todd," she said. With that, she opened the door of the main studio and stepped into the hall. Without a backward glance, she hurried down the corridor to the lobby.

Elizabeth took a deep breath and punched the button at the elevator bank. The mirrored doors opened almost immediately, revealing a full elevator of tall models wearing short skirts and long blazers, all gazing coolly ahead. Elizabeth gasped. All the models looked like carbon copies of Simone. She gritted her teeth and stepped inside. Her head throbbing, she leaned against the wall and closed her eyes. The elevator ride seemed to take forever.

When the elevator finally reached the ground floor, Elizabeth pushed her way out first.

"Well, *excuse* me," a pointed voice said.

"Interns," said another disgusted model.

But Elizabeth ignored the haughty voices of the fashion clones. She flew across the shiny marble floor of the huge, elegant lobby and pushed through the swinging doors to the sidewalk. She just wanted to get far away from *Flair* magazine and Todd and Simone as quickly as possible. Once outside, she took big gulps of fresh air. She yanked off her high-heeled pumps and held them by their straps in one hand, hurrying across the sidewalk in her stockings.

5

Elizabeth jumped into her Jeep and revved the engine. Then she tore out of the parking lot.

As she sped down the Santa Monica Freeway, Elizabeth unrolled the window and took long, haggard breaths, trying to calm herself. Normally she was a careful driver, but now she felt like throwing caution to the wind. She cut across the four-lane highway and darted into the left lane. The ground rushed underneath the wheels of the Jeep, echoing a strange rushing in her head. All week she'd had an eerie premonition, and finally it had come to pass. And it was worse than she'd ever imagined.

Elizabeth couldn't understand how everything had changed so quickly. In just a few days, Todd had gone from being a Sweet Valley High basketball star to a fashion model—and from her loyal boyfriend to a swinging playboy.

This week certainly hasn't turned out like I expected, Elizabeth thought dejectedly. As part of a new career program, Sweet Valley High juniors were taking part in a two-week-long internship program. Most of the students weren't taking it seriously. Todd hadn't bothered looking for an interesting position and had ended up as an assistant at his dad's software company, Varitronics. His job had consisted mostly of making copies and filing invoices. Jessica's best friend, Lila Fowler, hadn't done much better, filling in as a receptionist at Fowler Electronics, one of her father's computer chip companies.

Some of the students had been more entrepreneurial, though. Aaron Dallas had found a spot working for the general manager of the Lakers, and Winston Egbert was assisting the head chef of an exclusive gourmet Italian restaurant in Beverly Hills. Elizabeth's best friends Enid Rollins and Maria Slater had found perfect positions as well: Enid, who had a passion for literature, was acting as an intern at Morgan Literary Agency, and Maria, a former child actress, was serving as an assistant at the Bridgewater Theater Group in downtown Sweet Valley.

But Elizabeth and Jessica had landed the most exciting positions of all. They were interning at *Flair,* a hot new fashion magazine. *Flair* was less than two years old, but it was already the most popular publication of the Mode Magazine Group. Elizabeth was working in the editorial department of *Flair* as an assistant to Leona Peirson, the managing editor, and Jessica was working in the art department for the head photographer, Quentin Berg.

When she and Jessica had first heard about their internships, Elizabeth had been ecstatic. Even though Elizabeth wasn't exactly a fashion buff, she was thrilled to be learning the inner workings of a real magazine. And the job had surpassed her wildest dreams. Elizabeth had expected to do mostly grunt work—or "scum work," as Leona had called it. And while she had a fair amount of tedious chores to do—opening mail, making copies, and fact checking articles—Leona had entrusted her with some serious assignments. In the few days she'd been at *Flair,* Elizabeth had already drafted a letter, proofread sections of the magazine, and used the Library of Congress database to do research for an upcoming article. Not only that, but Elizabeth had her own plush office complete with a state-of-the-art computer and printer. She had thrown herself into her duties, and Leona had been so impressed with the results that she had mentioned the possibility of a summer job.

But then everything had changed. Fueled by her success, Elizabeth had done research on her own and had come up with a great idea for the magazine: an interactive reader-written article. Her idea was that the magazine would feature a one-page column called "Free Style" in which a reader of the month would write her personal opinions about fashion. Armed with a write-up of her research and notes, Elizabeth had presented the idea to Leona. Leona had flatly rejected it, explaining that it would bring down the quality of writing in the magazine. But she had promised to run the idea by the editor in chief. Elizabeth cringed at the memory. It was bad enough that Leona had rejected her idea, but it was even worse that she had condescended to her.

It began to drizzle, and wind whistled through the car. Elizabeth shivered and rolled up the window.

Then she caught sight of the familiar Sweet Valley exit sign on the far right. *Darn,* she muttered under her breath. Without bothering to put on her turn signal, she flew across the four lanes of the highway. A blue Toyota blared its horn and swerved out of her way, causing another car to screech on its brakes.

Elizabeth skidded onto the exit ramp and slowed down, shaking slightly. *Elizabeth Wakefield,* she reprimanded herself. *Get a hold of yourself.* The rain was coming down steadily now, and Elizabeth turned on the windshield wipers. Her life was falling apart but that was no reason to get in an accident.

Elizabeth stared gloomily ahead as she drove down the familiar winding roads of Sweet Valley. First her job turned out to be a failure, then her relationship. Elizabeth shook her head, feeling her cheeks burn again as the sight of Todd and the Fashion Witch, as Jessica called Simone, came back to her. Her life had gotten so bad so quickly. One moment Todd was sending her love-faxes from his internship at Varitronics, the next he was wrapped up in Simone's black widow spider arms.

Last Tuesday afternoon, Todd had stopped by unexpectedly to pick up Elizabeth, but she had been mired in work. So she had sent him down to the art department to entertain himself. *And entertain himself he did,* she thought bitterly.

Todd had walked in on a photo shoot with Simone that Quentin was directing. According to

Jessica, Quentin knew immediately that he wanted to photograph Todd's youthful face. And apparently Todd fell in love with Simone's *overexposed* face at the same moment. Quentin had taken a few test shots of Todd, and the next day he called to hire him as a model. Todd quit his internship at Varitronics to be the next big thing, and the rest was history.

Hot tears rolled down Elizabeth's cheeks as she pulled into the driveway of the Wakefield house on Calico Drive, and she wiped them away. It was just so humiliating. It didn't matter how interesting you were, it didn't matter how much character you had. What all guys really wanted were supermodels.

Jessica Wakefield stormed into the house after work, furious at Elizabeth. Her twin was supposed to give her a ride home, but when Jessica got to the parking lot, the Jeep was gone. So Jessica had to suffer rush hour traffic on two buses to get back to Sweet Valley. Plus, it was raining, and she had gotten soaked to the skin. It was one thing to be stranded at Sweet Valley High, but it was another to be stranded in downtown L.A.!

Jessica headed to the kitchen and threw her black leather bag on the counter. She was angry, she was hungry, and she was drenched. Jessica peeled off her wet blazer and shook out her damp hair. *It figures,* she thought. The weather had been clear and beautiful all week. Of course it had started to rain the one evening that Elizabeth decided to abandon her. Jessica didn't wear a watch, and she never carried an umbrella. That's what her twin was for. But apparently, her sister wasn't there for her anymore. A bolt of thunder rocked the house as if it were emphasizing Jessica's angry thoughts.

Swinging open the refrigerator door, Jessica uncapped a container of orange juice and drank directly from the bottle. Then she foraged hungrily through the fridge, grabbing a carton of yogurt, a bowl of cut vegetables, and a wedge of cheddar cheese. Balancing the food in one hand, she pulled a box of crackers from the cabinet and then dropped everything in a heap on the counter.

Jessica jumped up on a stool and munched aggressively on a baby carrot. She didn't know what had gotten into her sister. Normally Elizabeth was the responsible twin, and Jessica was the unpredictable one. Elizabeth was a straight A student with high ambitions to be a professional writer someday. A staff writer for the school newspaper, the *Oracle*, Elizabeth spent much of her time in the *Oracle* office working on her "Personal Profiles" column or writing feature articles. In her spare time, she preferred quiet pursuits, such as taking walks with her boyfriend, Todd, or going to the movies with her best friends, Enid and Maria. Fashion had never been a big priority for Elizabeth, and her looks tended toward the conservative. Elizabeth's signature attire was beige pants and a polo shirt or jeans and a cotton blouse.

Jessica, on the other hand, lived to make fashion statements. She was always at the forefront of new fads, and her taste bordered on the outrageous. Mini-miniskirts and wild colors suited her best. Jessica's personality matched her clothes. The co-captain of the cheerleading squad and an active member of Pi Beta Alpha, the most exclusive sorority at Sweet Valley High, Jessica was always at the center of the crowd. When she wasn't at cheerleading practice, she could usually be found in one of three places: the mall, the ocean, or the dance floor of the beach disco.

But ever since we've started our internships, Jessica thought, *Liz has become a totally different person.* Suddenly Elizabeth was only interested in fashion and success. She had entirely revamped her look with a chic new haircut and a brand-new professional wardrobe. After one day at work, Elizabeth took all the money she had been saving for a new computer and blew it on a shopping spree at the mall.

Jessica sighed. Elizabeth hadn't just undergone a physical transformation, but a personality transformation as well. Ever since she had started at *Flair,* she hadn't had a moment for Todd, or for Enid and Maria. Jessica cut off a wedge a cheese and sandwiched it between two crackers, biting into the concoction thoughtfully. It seemed as though considerate, polite Elizabeth Wakefield had turned into a power-hungry shark with an eye only for her own success.

Jessica's eyes narrowed. Her sister was definitely changing, and Jessica didn't like it one bit. *In fact,* Jessica thought worriedly, *Elizabeth is becoming more and more like me!* Jessica took a gulp of juice, shuddering at the thought. Despite their physical resemblance, from their silky golden blond hair to their blue-green eyes to their slim athletic figures, the two girls were so different on the inside that their friends could always tell them apart. Instead of competing for attention, they'd always complimented one other. And Jessica liked it that way. One Jessica was enough! After all, if Elizabeth started acting like her, then who was going to act like Elizabeth? Who was going to cover for Jessica when she needed it?

Jessica hopped off the stool and wiped crumbs from her skirt. It was time to give Elizabeth a piece of her mind. She had to straighten her out before it was too late.

With determination, Jessica marched up the stairs and down the hall. She burst into Elizabeth's room. "I can't believe you left me stranded in downtown L.A.!" she yelled. "It's one thing to blow off your friends, but I'm your *sister!* This is going too far! If you think—"

Jessica stopped midsentence. Elizabeth was lying facedown in her bed, sobbing her heart out. A big box of blue tissues sat next to her on the bed, with a mountain of crumbled tissues surrounding it.

Jessica's anger immediately turned to concern.

13

"Hey, what happened?" she asked, picking up the box and taking a seat next to Elizabeth on the bed.

Jessica's question only provoked a fresh outpouring of tears. "Shh . . . it's OK, it's OK," she said soothingly, rubbing her sister's back.

Finally, Elizabeth hiccuped and pulled herself up to a sitting position. Her face was red and blotchy, and her hair was in disarray. "It's Todd," Elizabeth choked out between tears. "He and—I saw—art department—*Simone*." She burst into tears again and grabbed a tissue, blowing her nose loudly.

Jessica's eyes widened. "You caught Todd with Simone?" she asked.

Elizabeth nodded, a rivulet of tears streaming down her cheeks.

"That is so *despicable*," Jessica declared. She brushed back a long lock of hair from Elizabeth's cheek and tucked it behind her ear.

Elizabeth nodded and sniffed, wiping at her eyes. "I'm not surprised about the Stick," she said. "But T-Todd—" She waved a hand in the air.

Jessica nodded. "I think this modeling thing has gone to his head." She was about to say that it was all for the best, since boring-as-butter Todd Wilkins was a total drip, but she bit back her words. Now was clearly not the time.

Elizabeth brought her knees up to her chest and wrapped her arms around them. "Jess, I'm sorry," she said. "I went to the art department to find Todd, and when I saw him with Simone, I just freaked out and ran. I was so upset that I forgot about giving you a ride." Fresh tears came to her eyes.

"Hey, you're going to drown if you keep this up!" Jessica said, scooting back across the bed and leaning against the wall next to Elizabeth. "Now don't worry about it," she said, propping a throw pillow behind her sister's back and placing a comforting arm around her shoulders. "There's nothing I'd rather do on a Thursday night than take public transportation in the rain."

Elizabeth smiled through her tears. "You're the best, Jess," she said. Then she closed her eyes and rested her head back on the pillow.

Jessica narrowed her eyes, her anger displaced from Elizabeth to Simone. Ever since Jessica had met the superskinny, supersnobby supermodel, she had known there would be trouble. Simone was a spoiled prima donna who thought she was the center of the universe. And as the photographer's assistant, Jessica was at Simone's beck and call—which meant fetching mineral water and celery sticks and supplying her with a constant supply of outfits and props.

It was bad enough that Simone had been treating Jessica like dirt, ordering her around and making ridiculous demands. Messing with *her* was one thing. Jessica could defend herself. But moving in on her twin's boyfriend was something else altogether. Simone was going to pay.

Chapter 2

It was only nine P.M., but Elizabeth lay in bed, tossing and turning. The picture of Todd together with Simone kept dancing before her eyes, tormenting her. Elizabeth flipped on her side and wrapped the covers around herself, trying to shake the image from her mind. Outside, rain was pouring steadily down. Usually the sounds of rain soothed her, but tonight it just added to her anxiety.

Think of the ocean, she told herself. She concentrated deeply, imagining the picturesque view at Ocean Bay. She saw hot, white sand and the foamy blue-green sea. White-capped breakers crashed onto the shore, and seagulls cut arcing patterns above the waves. Then she saw Todd and Simone walking hand in hand along the shore. Simone was barefoot and carrying her sandals in one hand, but her storklike legs were so long that she was almost as tall as Todd. *I can't believe you took her to the beach,* Elizabeth irrationally told Todd in her mind. *Our beach.* . . . Pain stabbed at her heart.

Elizabeth shook her head and threw off the covers, sitting up in bed. It was no use. She couldn't sleep. She couldn't stop thinking about Todd and Simone. Sighing deeply, she reached over and turned on the lamp next to her bed. The first thing she saw was a copy of *Flair* on her nightstand. Leona had given her a stack of back issues so she could familiarize herself with the magazine, and this one featured a barely bikini-clad Simone. Elizabeth sucked in her breath, feeling assaulted by the photograph.

She picked up the magazine and examined the cover. Usually pictures of models in bathing suits offended her feminist sensibility, but this one was particularly artistic. It had clearly been shot by Quentin Berg. The photo was in black and white, with a grainy quality that gave it a dated look. Elizabeth had to admit that Simone looked good. She was perched on a white boulder, her long legs folded gracefully underneath her. Her sleek asymmetrically-cut jet black hair provided a sharp contrast to her flawless ivory skin. Her full lips were pursed together in a pout, and her pale and strangely blank eyes stared directly at the camera. She was obviously beautiful, but she seemed empty—and cold. And she was so skinny that she looked like a starvation victim. But

17

obviously, that's what Todd wanted. He didn't want someone with life. He wanted someone with status. Supermodel status.

Elizabeth scowled, feeling like a nobody, a nothing. She felt like her entire self had been made worthless. She could change her interests, but she couldn't change her looks. She'd never be six feet tall. She'd never look like a supermodel. Elizabeth balled her hands into fists, seething with frustration. Then she tore off the cover of the magazine, ripping it into tiny pieces. She threw the pieces on the floor, watching in satisfaction as they scattered over her cream-colored carpet.

Elizabeth slid out of bed and kicked at the torn pieces on the floor, crushing Simone's lips into the carpet with her heel. She paced from one side of her bedroom to the other, grinding her teeth. She stopped at the door and surveyed her room, itching with dissatisfaction. It was so impeccably neat and orderly. She looked in disgust at her perfectly clean desk with her reference books and computer, at her armoire with her shoes all lined up, at the tidy bookshelves. . . . Her room used to give her a sense of peace and a desire to work. Now she felt caged in. Elizabeth yanked open a window, letting in a gust of cold, windy air. Then she grabbed her clothes from the bed and threw them on the floor in a heap.

Maybe it's all my fault, Elizabeth thought, pushing her clothes out of the way with her foot as she crossed the room again. After all, she *had* been neglecting Todd. Ever since she had found out about her internship, the job had been the only thing on her mind. Todd had called her—and faxed her—and had even driven all the way to L.A. to see her. But she hadn't given him a second of her time.

Then Elizabeth dismissed the thought as ridiculous. When Todd had trained like a madman for the basketball finals last season, she had barely seen him at all. And she had understood. Besides, this internship was just two weeks long. Just because Todd hadn't bothered looking for an interesting position was no reason Elizabeth shouldn't try to make a future for herself.

Elizabeth grabbed a woolen blanket from her bed and flopped dejectedly onto her pale velvet divan. She couldn't believe that all these years could be erased in a second—in a kiss. Todd was her constant companion, her other half. It seemed like they'd always been together. And Elizabeth had thought they'd *always* be together.

A jumble of random memories flooded into her mind, causing her chest to constrict in pain. She remembered seeing Todd at basketball practice the week before, wearing cutoff blue sweatpants and a canary yellow T-shirt. She'd stopped by to see him after school, and he'd turned and sent her a kiss, mouthing "I love you" in the air. She saw his brown eyes staring at her intensely at Miller's Point, a popular parking spot high above Sweet

Valley. And then she saw herself and Todd together in the park one afternoon years ago, when they had shared their first, tentative kiss. . . .

Elizabeth curled her legs underneath her and wrapped her blanket around her shoulders. She didn't know how she was going to make it through the school year. Sweet Valley was full of too many memories. She reached over and picked up the framed picture of Todd from her bookshelf. He was smiling at her, and his deep brown eyes were warm and trusting. She quickly put it back, laying it face down on the shelf. *How could you throw it all away, Todd?* she thought in pain, hot tears coming to her eyes. *How could you betray me like this? How could you betray us like this?*

Tears trickled down her cheeks, and she jumped up, brushing them angrily away. She couldn't let herself go to pieces. After all, she still had her pride. It was bad enough that Todd had fallen in love with someone else, but he had cheated on her—at her own workplace. Elizabeth shook her head in disgust. She had thought that Todd was different from other guys. She had thought he cared about things that really mattered. But no, as soon as a supermodel walked into the vicinity, he was history.

A flash of lightning illuminated the sky and a blast of rain shot through the open window. Shivering, Elizabeth pulled the window shut. Then she prowled across the room, feeling restless. She didn't know what to do with herself. She wanted to talk to someone. Jessica was wonderful, but she needed a friend who would truly understand her situation—like Enid. Enid always managed to make her feel better. She was levelheaded and could always give Elizabeth a sense of perspective about things.

Picking the phone up from her nightstand, she carried it to the floor and plopped down on the carpet, bringing her knees up to her chest. She punched in Enid's number, waiting as the phone rang. But no one answered, and she hung up when Mrs. Rollins's answering machine picked up.

Elizabeth blinked back tears, feeling a little desperate for support. She stared at the number pad, wondering if she should call Maria. She had been giving her friends the brush-off lately, and they were probably mad at her. But then again, they were her best friends. They would understand. They would be there for her.

Without thinking about it any further, Elizabeth quickly dialed Maria's number. She twisted the phone cord around her finger as the phone rang. *Maria, please be there*, she thought.

Finally Maria picked up. "Yes?" she asked, her voice giddy. Elizabeth breathed a sigh of relief.

"Maria, it's Elizabeth," she said.

"Oh, hi, Elizabeth," Maria responded, her voice turning distinctly cold. Elizabeth winced. Then she heard giggling in the background.

"Is this a bad time?" Elizabeth asked. "Is somebody over?" She twisted the phone cord tighter in her hand, nearly cutting off the circulation in her fingers.

"Enid is staying over tonight," Maria explained, her voice clipped and distant. "We're helping each other out with stuff for our internships."

"Oh," Elizabeth said softly, hit with a pang of jealousy. Enid and Maria never used to hang out without her. "Why didn't you invite me?" she asked, trying to keep the hurt out of her voice.

"Hmm," Maria said. "Just a minute." Elizabeth could tell she had covered the receiver with her hand, but her muffled voice came through anyway. "Enid, Elizabeth wants to know why we didn't invite her over." Elizabeth heard the girls giggle, and tears welled up in her eyes again. What was going on? Was the whole world turning on her?

Enid got on the phone a moment later. "Hi, Elizabeth, it's Enid," she said.

"Hi," Elizabeth replied tentatively.

Enid's voice was cold. "In answer to your question, we weren't aware that you'd have time to hang out with two peons like us. You've been so busy with the power players that we didn't want to disturb you."

Elizabeth didn't even have the energy to respond. She said good-bye quietly and hung up the phone.

Elizabeth wrapped her arms around her body, feeling worse than she had before. She was completely alone in the world. First she lost Todd. Now she'd lost her two best friends.

The rain pelted down around her, enveloping her in her solitude.

"What horrible weather!" Enid exclaimed later that evening as she and Maria ducked out of the beating rain into the Dairi Burger, Sweet Valley's most popular teenage hangout. Enid shivered as she took off her raincoat and hung it up on a peg.

Maria closed her dilapidated umbrella with difficulty and then dropped it into the bucket by the door. "I don't know why I bothered bringing that," Maria said, looking down at the umbrella in dismay. It was so windy that the umbrella had turned inside out, and the girls had gotten soaked during the short walk from the parking lot to the restaurant. A bolt of thunder rocked the sky, and a gust of cool wind shot through the door.

Enid pushed the door shut and wrapped her olive green cardigan sweater tightly around herself. "Let's take a booth in the back," she suggested. "It'll be warmer farther away from the door."

Despite the bad weather, the restaurant was hopping. The booths were jammed with students talking and laughing in groups. *Pings* and *bleeps* sounded from the game room.

Enid headed for a booth in back, Maria a step behind her. A series of whistles and catcalls followed in their wake.

"Lookin' good!" Bruce Patman, the richest and most arrogant student at Sweet Valley High, called out.

"Foxy mama!" yelled out Paul Jeffries.

Enid turned to see the commotion. A bunch of senior guys at a corner table were staring at Maria, practically drooling.

Enid shook her head. "Looks like you're creating a stir, as usual," she said with a grin. "You've still got that movie star aura."

Maria rolled her eyes. "Oh, come on," she scoffed, taking Enid's arm and hurrying her to the back. "Toilet paper commercials do not a movie star make."

Even though Maria looked like a movie star, Enid knew she didn't want to be treated like one. Maria had been a successful film and commercial actress as a child. But when she hit puberty, the roles had stopped coming. Her family had recently moved back to Sweet Valley from New York, and now she wanted more than anything to be a normal teenager.

"Well, you *do* look pretty chic," Enid said, glancing at her friend admiringly. With her funky retro look, Maria had a style all her own. Tonight she was wearing a pale blue forties dress with huge square buttons and thick army boots on her feet. An exotic green silk scarf was tied over her head, hiding her hair completely. "Maybe *you* should be interning at *Flair* magazine."

"Ugh," Maria groaned, sliding into the booth

24

opposite Enid. She pulled off her scarf and ran a finger through her short-cropped dark curly hair. "Don't even *mention* that name." She shivered and wrapped the scarf around her neck, tying it adeptly at the back.

Enid shook her head. "I don't know what's gotten into Elizabeth lately."

A waiter appeared at their table, and the girls quickly placed their orders—fries and shakes for both of them.

Maria spoke in a low voice after the waiter had left. "You know, I'm worried about Elizabeth—she isn't acting like herself."

"You can say that again," Enid agreed. "She's acting like some self-centered fashion plate. I would say that she's turned into Jessica—but in this case, that's being kind."

Maria frowned. "I don't know, Enid. Maybe something's going on that we don't know about. I've known Elizabeth forever, and I've never seen her act like this. She's not usually inconsiderate— or egotistical. And she's *never* been interested in fashion."

It's true, Enid thought. Usually Elizabeth was a totally loyal friend, and Enid could always count on her. But ever since she'd gotten her internship, Elizabeth had become an entirely different person. She was preoccupied, and all she talked about was herself. She had completely ignored Enid and Maria all week, and Wednesday night had been the last

25

straw. In order to make up for neglecting them, Elizabeth had invited them to meet her in L.A. to go to a cappuccino bar after work. Enid and Maria had endured two bus rides and three traffic jams to meet Elizabeth downtown, only to find that Elizabeth couldn't make it because her boss wanted her to stay late. Elizabeth hadn't even been the slightest bit apologetic. Enid and Maria had been furious.

The waiter set down strawberry shakes and two plates of fries in front of them. Enid squeezed out a mound of ketchup on her plate and grabbed a few fries hungrily.

Maria bit her lip. "Maybe we should invite her to meet us tonight," she said thoughtfully. "She sounded upset on the phone." She pulled the wrapper off her straw and took a long draw on her shake.

Enid looked at her friend in shock. "Maria, are you crazy? Did you forget about Wednesday night already?"

Maria shrugged, dragging a fry through Enid's ketchup. "Well, we had fun anyway."

After Elizabeth ditched them, Enid and Maria decided to make the best of being in L.A. They had strolled down Rodeo Drive and peeked in all the shops. Then they had gotten their pictures taken in a color photo booth and had gone dancing at an underage club. The teenage crowd had been a bit too superficial for their tastes, but they'd had a fantastic evening anyway.

"Hey, that reminds me," Enid said, her eyes lighting up. "There's a guy at my literary agency who saw the pictures we took in the booth the other day. His name is Shane Maddox, he's an editorial assistant, and he's dying to meet you."

Maria shook her head, waggling a fry at Enid. "Forget it. After my disastrous date with Kevin yesterday, I'm swearing off all guys. At least guys I don't know."

Kevin Anderson was the set manager at the theater, and they'd gone out for lunch to an artsy little bistro. Maria had been talking about her date for days, but it turned out they had nothing in common. She'd said they spent an hour talking about California weather.

Enid shrugged. "Oh, well, too bad. Because Shane's pret-ty cu-ute."

"What does he look like?" Maria asked. "Just out of curiosity," she added quickly.

Enid crossed her legs and leaned back in the booth. "Well, let's see. He's about six feet tall, broad-shouldered, and handsome. *Plus*, he has beautiful ebony skin." Enid knew that the last detail would get Maria. Even though her friend didn't prefer any single type, she had a soft spot for really dark-skinned guys.

Maria's eyes widened, but Enid waved a dismissive hand in the air. "Oh, well . . . too bad. I'll just tell him you're not interested."

Maria refused to rise to the bait. "OK," she said with a smug smile.

"Hmmph," Enid pouted, drumming her fingers on the wooden table.

Maria laughed and leaned in closer to Enid. "But, on the other hand, I think I might have a guy for you."

"Oh yeah, who?" Enid asked, dipping a spoon into her strawberry shake. She was trying to sound nonchalant, but actually, she was thrilled. Ever since her obsession with Jonathan Cain, a deranged transfer student who had been at Sweet Valley for a month, her life had been entirely guyless.

"Kevin, the set manager."

"What?" Enid sputtered. "The guy you went out with yesterday?"

Maria grinned. "What's wrong? You don't like to share?"

"Forget it, Maria," Enid said firmly. "If Kevin's interested in you, then he won't be interested in me. There's no way I'm going out with him. Absolutely *no way*."

"Enid, I'm telling you, it didn't click between us," Maria insisted. "We had *nothing* in common. Zero. Zilch. There was no spark at all."

Enid's eyes narrowed. "Well, maybe not for you."

Maria laughed. "Honestly, he wasn't interested either." Then she turned her sly almond-shaped eyes to Enid. "Actually, I told him a little bit about you. He said you sounded really interesting and that he'd like to get to know you better."

28

Enid shook her head. "Well, I'm not interested. I do not compete with Maria Slater, former child actress. *Period*." She dipped a spoon into her shake and brought a spoonful of ice cream to her mouth.

Maria frowned. "Hmm. There's just one little problem. I sort of told him you were free Friday night."

Enid choked on her ice cream. "You—*what*?"

"Well, aren't you?" Maria pressed.

Enid shook her head. "Maria Slater, you are totally outrageous. I am going on that date on one condition and one condition only."

"And what is that?" Maria asked with a grin.

"That you come along—with Shane Maddox."

Maria grimaced. "A double blind date?"

Enid shrugged. "It's that or nothing."

"OK, you're on," Maria agreed with a laugh.

Jessica sat cross-legged in bed late Thursday night, turning the pages of the latest issue of *Ingenue*. She stopped at a spread covering upcoming spring fashions and studied the chic models featured in it. They were all blondes, with hazel eyes and fair complexions, and they were all wearing short dresses in shades of green and orange. Even though the women had similar coloring, each of them seemed to have a unique, individual look. *Some day, that will be me*, Jessica thought happily. *Some day soon. . . .*

Jessica hugged her arms around her body,

thinking excitedly about her future as a super-model. In just one day, her entire life had turned around. And it was all because of Quentin Berg, the hotshot photographer she was working for at *Flair*.

Quentin, who was under contract to *Flair*, was one of the biggest names in the fashion business. He was in his early twenties, with shaggy blond hair, broad shoulders, and deep, mysterious gray eyes. He was good-looking in a rumpled, artistic kind of way, but he wasn't really Jessica's type. Jessica liked a tougher, more masculine look. But Jessica was determined to charm him, because Quentin could help her advance her career as a model.

At first, Quentin had treated her like dirt. For the most part, he had acted like she wasn't on the set at all. And when he did notice her, it was just to snarl at her. He had basically been a total jerk, ordering her to get him coffee and pick up his prints at the mail room.

But then everything had changed. Driven to extreme measures, Jessica had stolen one of Quentin's cameras, a state-of-the-art Minolta with a telephoto lens, and had coerced Lila into taking pictures of her at the beach. Lila had shot two roles of film with Jessica cavorting on the water's edge, but unfortunately the camera had ended up in the ocean as well.

When Quentin discovered that his camera was

missing, he had been livid, and Jessica had done her best to avoid him. But out of nowhere a brand new camera had mysteriously appeared in its spot, with a note from Jessica saying she had given it a thorough overhaul and cleaning. At first, Jessica had been baffled. But then she realized that Lila must have secretly replaced the camera for her.

After that, Quentin had warmed up. He had even begun to notice her work and had complimented her efforts with the sets. And then Jessica had made her move. Wednesday night after work, she had snuck into the darkroom and approached Quentin from behind, giving him a mysterious kiss and then disappearing into the night. When he saw her at work the next day, he was clearly intrigued, but Jessica just smiled enigmatically. Then she had shown him her photos. He had been impressed and had invited her to dinner—to discuss her potential as a fashion model.

Jessica's stomach tightened in excitement. Tomorrow could be the start of her career as the newest supermodel on the fashion scene.

Not only had Quentin made a 360-degree turnaround at work, but so had Cameron Smith, a cute guy who worked in the mailroom. Jessica propped up her pillow and sat back against the wall, thinking dreamily of her encounters with Cameron. The first time she had met him, she had been dozing on a couch in the mailroom. He had kissed her awake like the prince in *Sleeping Beauty*. His gallantry had continued after that, and he had made his interest in her clear.

But, bent on advancing her career through Quentin, Jessica had steadily avoided Cameron, and eventually he had figured that out. "You're only interested in people with classy titles or flashy cars or tons of money!" he had spat at her this morning. Jessica had finally convinced him he was wrong. And this afternoon, he had found her alone in the wardrobe room and kissed her in a way that she'd never been kissed. Then he'd asked her out for Friday night.

Jessica leaned back against her pillow, reliving his passionate kiss. She could feel his strong arms wrapped around her and smell his deep, masculine scent. She shivered again as she remembered the fountain of sparks that had cascaded over her entire body. Jessica closed her eyes contentedly. She didn't know how she'd make it to Friday night.

That she bolted upright. *Friday night!* That's when she was supposed to go out with Quentin. *I knew it was too good to be true,* she thought dejectedly. *I knew my life couldn't completely change in one day.* Now she had to make a choice—between a dream guy and a dream career.

Jessica sighed and climbed into bed. It was an impossible dilemma. She couldn't give up Cameron or her chance to become a model. Jessica pulled the covers tightly around her. *How can I possibly choose?*

❖　　❖　　❖

Todd took Simone's hand and spun her around at the center of the dance floor. It was almost midnight, and he and Simone were at the Edge, a hip new nightclub in downtown L.A. This was the latest he'd ever been out on a school night. The dance floor was packed with a chichi L.A. crowd, and loud techno music blasted from the speakers. Todd felt his head whirling with the pulsing beat of the electronic music.

"This is what it's like living on the edge, Todd," Simone whispered in a husky voice in his ear. "How do you like it?"

Todd shrugged. "No big deal," he said, trying to sound cool. But his voice came out as a squeak, and he blushed.

Simone grinned. "You are so *cute,* Todd," she squealed. Todd's blush deepened, but Simone was already turning her attention to the other side of the room. "Look," she said, pointing an elegant finger at the bar. "That's Sven Sorensen, the editor in chief of *Ingenue* magazine."

Todd followed her gaze. A lanky, Swedish-looking man with a blond beard was sitting at the bar with a group of tall models crowded around him.

Todd nodded, searching in vain for something intelligent to say. Then he realized that Simone wasn't paying attention anyway. She was too busy posing for Sven. She steered herself and Todd around so Sven could get a view of her profile. "Spin me, Todd," she commanded in an intense voice. Todd swung her around obediently, and she twirled wildly, trying to get Sven's attention.

Todd blushed, feeling more self-conscious than ever. He could see every guy in the place looking at him with total envy because he was with Simone. He was wearing jeans and a T-shirt, and he wished he'd worn something a little more hip. The crowd was made up of chic actors and models, and they were all dressed almost entirely in black. The women were wearing short skirts or tight dresses, and most of the guys had on black jeans and funky retro jackets.

Sven stood up from the bar, and Simone stopped midspin. "Oh, I'll be right back," she said, her voice breathless. Then she rushed off.

Todd stood in the middle of the dance floor. He tried to make out Simone through the crowd, but gyrating bodies blocked his view. There were a few couples on the dance floor, but most of the people were dancing alone, swaying to the music as if they were in a trance.

"Hey, you wanna join the love parade?" a sultry voice whispered in his ear.

"Huh?" Todd said, blinking. He turned to see a woman with short scarlet hair standing by his side. She had a nosering and a lipring. A trail of dancers followed her in a line, bobbing rhythmically in an almost hypnotic state.

"It's a communion with Being," she said. "You close your eyes and let the music fill your body."

"C'mon, get in line," urged a blond woman with a silver streak in her hair. "You'll see. It's a natural high."

"Uh, no thanks," Todd said quickly. "I was just going to get a drink."

He waved and walked away, the eerie sound of the women's laughter echoing in his ears. Weaving through the grinding bodies, he quickly made his way to the bar.

"What'll you have?" the bartender barked. He was a bulky man with a huge grizzly beard.

Todd gulped. He was tempted to order a drink, but he was underage. If he got carded, he would get kicked out of the club and would be totally humiliated.

"Just a mineral water," he said quickly.

The bartender nodded and picked up a bottle of seltzer. He poured the bubbling water into a tall glass.

Todd picked up his drink and leaned against the bar, taking in the surroundings. The club was done in ultramodern decor, with stark white tables and shiny black floors. A red, flashing neon band surrounded the wall, and a shimmering disco ball hung over the middle of the dance floor. The hip L.A. crowd looked as electric as the club itself.

Todd took a sip of his drink, feeling entirely out of place. He wondered if anybody knew he was underage. He was trying to play it cool, but he felt as if he were wearing a huge sign on his back that screamed Sixteen!

"Oh, Todd, there you are!" Simone breathed by his side. "C'mon, let's go back to the dance floor," she said, taking his hand.

"Sure," Todd agreed, downing his drink and following her back to the floor. He definitely preferred the dance floor to the bar. Dancing was one thing he could legitimately do. At the bar, he felt like a total fraud.

Simone wrapped her arms around his waist and pressed her body to his.

Todd coughed uncomfortably, shifting back a few inches. "So, did you have any luck with the editor in chief of *Ingenue*?" he asked.

Simone nodded in pleasure. "He's going to call me," she said. "He wants to use me for the cover of the next issue." She giggled gleefully. "That means I'll be replacing Justine Laroche. She's going to be *green*."

"Hey, that's great," Todd said, trying to sound happy for her. *I just can't think of a modeling job as important,* he thought. Then he swallowed hard, suddenly struck by how hypocritical he was being. This was his crowd now. *He* was a model too.

Todd looked at the beautiful people around him and tried to convince himself that he was having a great time—and that the nagging feeling in the pit of his stomach had nothing to do with Elizabeth. He decided that he must be allergic to the shrimp cocktail he and Simone had eaten earlier.

Then, out of the corner of his eye, he glimpsed

a blond girl across the dance floor. For a split second his heart leapt. *Elizabeth!* he thought. Maybe she had come here to find him—to reconcile with him. But then the girl turned. It wasn't Elizabeth. Simone pulled him closer in her arms.

A wave of disappointment washed over him, and suddenly Elizabeth's bitter words came back to him. *You're not the person I thought you were.* Todd felt a sharp pang in his heart.

Then he shook off his negative feelings. Obviously Elizabeth was right: He wasn't just a normal teenager. He was *model* material. He was meant for fame and fortune. It was going to be difficult to leave his old life behind, but he'd have to get used to it. He'd have to rise to the challenge.

I'm happy to be in Simone's arms, he told himself. *Very, very happy.*

Chapter 3

Todd was alone at a nightclub with supermodels, and techno music was pounding in his brain. Rap rap rap, the pulsing musical beat throbbed. Rap rap rap. The girls were getting thinner and thinner and taller and taller and the music was getting louder and louder. "Wanna join the love parade?" a husky voice on his left asked. "Wanna join the love parade?" a voice on his right echoed. Suddenly Todd felt like he was going to go mad. He looked around for a way out of the club, but all he saw were grotesquely smooth and angular made-up faces looming in on him.

Todd moaned and opened his eyes, trying to orient himself. Then the sound repeated itself. Rap rap rap.

Todd's head was aching, and the beats of music merged with the pounding in his temples. He held his head, trying to place the sound. Then the evening came back to him. *Simone. The Edge.* He squinted at the digital clock on the nightstand. *Eight o'clock.* He had slept through his alarm.

Todd groaned, realizing he felt lousy. His head was throbbing, and his whole body ached. *This must be what it feels like to have a hangover,* he thought, punching the blankets around him and burrowing deeper into his covers. He felt like staying inside all day. The prospect of getting out of his warm bed seemed overwhelming—and nearly impossible.

I shouldn't have stayed out so late with Simone, he thought with regret. He hadn't even had a good time. He had felt completely out of place.

Then the rapping sound came again, and Todd realized it was coming from the door. "C'mon in," he croaked out in a groggy voice.

His father stuck his head into Todd's room. "Be downstairs in two minutes," Mr. Wilkins ordered in an authoritative tone. Then he turned and marched away. Todd groaned. His dad did *not* sound happy.

Todd slid out of bed, rubbing his eyes wearily as he headed for the shower. This day was not starting out well. And he had a sinking feeling that it was only going to get worse.

When Todd turned down the hall to the kitchen, he saw his mom and dad waiting for him at the table. They were both dressed for work, and they were sitting perfectly still, like two wax figures. Emily Wilkins, a management consultant, had on a forest green wool suit that complimented her short glossy auburn hair and deep green eyes. In his plaid blue shirt, wine-colored tie, and blue suspenders, Bert Wilkins looked every bit the executive. The round wooden kitchen table was covered with a bright yellow tablecloth, and a platter of scrambled eggs stood in the middle. Todd's seat was empty and waiting for him, a bowl of cereal and a glass of orange juice set out on a place mat in front of it.

Todd hesitated at the doorway. Everything looked too ordinary. Something was definitely up. What was going on? Did his parents know he went out last night? He had gotten home around two in the morning and had snuck in the back door. But nobody had stirred. He had even peeked his head into his parents' room, and they had both been fast asleep.

His mother caught sight of him at the door. "Good morning, Todd," she said with a tight smile.

"Uh, morning," Todd mumbled, heading for the table. He sat down at his seat and stared at the tablecloth. Then he grabbed a piece of toast from the plate in the middle of the table and took a bite. The sounds of his chewing reverberated oddly in the silent room.

Bert Wilkins took a sip of black coffee. "You mother went grocery shopping this morning," he said.

Todd glanced at his father warily. He had definitely entered an alternate universe.

"And I picked up this copy of *Los Angeles Living*," Mrs. Wilkins put in, holding up a newspaper for Todd to see. *Los Angeles Living* was a tabloid paper that came out daily. Todd glanced at the paper in confusion. His mother never read junk like that.

"Uh-huh," Todd said warily, feeling as if he was being lead into a trap. Usually his parents were relaxed and casual at breakfast. Normally, his dad would be making jokes, and his mother would be asking Todd questions about school and his love life. Today they were acting so civilized that it was weird. It was like the calm before the storm.

Then Todd focused in on the picture on the cover and almost choked on his toast. It was a large color photo of himself and Simone on the dance floor at the Edge. Todd's mouth dropped open. Underneath the photo, a caption read, "Supermodel Simone and playboy Todd Wilkins danced till dawn."

"Are you aware that you have a curfew?" Mr. Wilkins asked in an ominous voice.

Todd gulped. He was in *big* trouble.

Elizabeth dragged herself into the *Flair* office on Friday morning after a sleepless night. For the first time since her internship had started, she didn't feel excited about the day ahead of her.

After tossing and turning for hours the night before, she'd finally managed to fall asleep. And then visions of Todd and Simone had haunted her dreams.

Elizabeth stared at the computer, wondering how she was going to get any work done. Then her eyes lit on the fax that Todd had sent her a few days ago. It was a cartoon of a guy and a girl in their respective offices. Above the boy's head was a dialogue bubble that read, "Your office or mine?" *Mine,* Elizabeth whispered aloud. *Right office, wrong girl.* Elizabeth ripped the fax off the wall and crumpled it in a ball, tossing it into the waste basket in disgust.

She cupped her fingers around her steaming mug of coffee, sighing deeply. It was bad enough that Todd was cheating on her with Simone. But they were both working at *Flair* as well. Elizabeth rubbed a weary eye. She didn't know how she was going to make it through the next week.

Elizabeth lifted her coffee mug to her lips, hoping to send a jolt of caffeine to the energy centers in her brain. But before she could take a sip, a head popped through her doorway. It was Reggie Andrews, an assistant fashion editor of the magazine.

"Good morning!" Reggie said, a smile lighting up her delicate features. A young Asian woman with fine black hair and a flawless complexion, Reggie was Elizabeth's closest friend at *Flair*. She had just started working at *Flair* after graduating college the year before and had filled in Elizabeth on all the ins and outs of the publishing world.

"Morning," Elizabeth responded in a lackluster tone.

"Uh-oh," Reggie said, her dark brown, almond-shaped eyes filled with concern. "You look like you just lost your best friend."

Elizabeth set down her coffee cup. "That too."

"Hey, what happened?" Reggie asked. She quickly took a seat in the chair opposite the desk.

But Elizabeth just shook her head. "I can't talk about it in the office," she said, her voice coming out as a whisper.

"Why don't we take a quick trip to the cappuccino bar for a cup of coffee?" Reggie suggested.

"I've already got coffee," Elizabeth said, pointing to her mug.

"Not anymore," Reggie responded. She stood up and picked up Elizabeth's mug off the desk. Then she flung the contents into the potted plant in the corner.

Elizabeth couldn't help smiling at Reggie's behavior.

"Ah! There we go! Got a smile out of her," Reggie said, clapping her hands lightly. "Now come on." She waved a hand in the air. "Get up."

Elizabeth stood up reluctantly. "OK," she agreed.

Reggie linked arms with her and lead her down the hall to the elevator, chatting all the way. "I have the feeling I never left this office," she said with a moan. "I was here until nine P.M. last night proof-reading the fashion features for this month's issue. And then I had to fact check all the info for the Milan runway show."

"Wow," Elizabeth said in appreciation as they stepped into the elevator. "That's a lot of work for one day." Elizabeth knew that Reggie was a top-notch editor. That's why she had gotten promoted to assistant editor after one year of working at *Flair*.

"You're telling me," Reggie said. "Sometimes I think I live here."

They got out at the first floor and crossed the elegant lobby. Then they hurried around the corner to Café Costa, a hip, new cappuccino bar. The coffee bar was almost deserted, and Reggie and Elizabeth walked right up to the counter.

"Double mocha cappuccinos for both of us," Reggie ordered. Then she turned to Elizabeth with a smile. "My treat."

Elizabeth returned her smile gratefully. Reggie was really a wonderful friend. After losing Todd, Enid, and Maria all in one night, it was nice to have a sympathetic ear.

"Here you go," Reggie said, handing her a steaming tall cup of coffee. "Why don't we sit down for a minute?"

Elizabeth hesitated. She knew she shouldn't take a break at the beginning of the day, but she was anxious to share her troubles with somebody.

"What if Leona needs me?" she asked worriedly.

"The dragon lady will have to wait," Reggie declared.

Reggie didn't share Elizabeth's high opinion of Leona Peirson. For some reason, Reggie didn't trust the managing editor at all. But Reggie couldn't really come up with a reason for her suspicions. "Women's intuition," she had said.

They took their seats on stools at a high round table in the corner by the window. "So what happened?" Reggie asked. She ripped open a package of brown sugar and poured it in her coffee.

Elizabeth took a deep breath. "It's Todd," she said. Her heart constricted, and she felt tears spring to her eyes. "He's—he's going out with Simone."

Reggie looked shocked. "With *Simone?* The Fashion Fink?"

"Shh!" Elizabeth cautioned, looking around wildly. But nobody was within earshot.

Reggie leaned in closer. "Elizabeth, are you sure? Maybe it's just a rumor. From what you've told me about Todd, he doesn't seem to be the type to go for flaky supermodels."

"Positive," Elizabeth said with a sigh. "I saw them with my own eyes. Yesterday after work—in the photography studio." She took a sip of her mocha coffee.

Reggie's eyes widened. "But what's gotten into him? Is he mad at you for something?"

45

Elizabeth nodded. "Yeah. He thinks I've been ignoring him." She picked up her napkin and shredded it. "It's all my fault," she said sadly, scattering the pieces on the table. "I shouldn't have given him the brush-off. I practically pushed him into Simone's arms."

But Reggie shook her head firmly. "It is absolutely *not* your fault," she countered. "Todd is his own person. He must not have much strength of character if he can be seduced so easily by a stupid model."

Elizabeth nodded. She knew Reggie was right. If a little bit of neglect could make Todd turn to other girls, then he wasn't worth her time—and then this relationship wasn't worth her time either.

"Look on the bright side," Reggie went on. "It's good that you found out what Todd's like now—before it's too late. Now you can find someone who *really* appreciates you."

Elizabeth nodded, but Reggie's words fell flat. There wasn't a bright side.

Elizabeth shut her office door and locked it, feeling dangerously close to tears. Somehow Reggie's sympathy had only made her feel worse. She wasn't ready to give up Todd. It wasn't a relief to find out that he wasn't the person she had always thought he was. It was a shock—a horrible shock.

Suddenly the phone jangled.

Elizabeth groaned, blinking back her tears. She took a deep breath to compose herself. Then she picked up the receiver. "Elizabeth Wakefield," she said.

Leona Peirson's voice came through the phone. "Could you come see me for a moment in my office?" she asked.

"Sure, Leona," Elizabeth said, trying to infuse her voice with some enthusiasm. "I'll be right there."

After redirecting her calls to the reception desk, Elizabeth grabbed a pen and tucked a yellow memo pad underneath her arm. She sighed as she crossed the plush gray carpet leading to Leona's spacious office. Unfortunately, she was going to have to tell Leona about Todd. She and Leona had made plans to go on a double date that evening. She bit her lip, wondering if Leona already knew that Elizabeth had been replaced by a supermodel. After all, news traveled fast on the *Flair* grapevine. Elizabeth's tongue went dry at the thought. She didn't think she could handle public humiliation on top of her broken heart.

Leona's voice carried down the hall, and Elizabeth hesitated at the door of the managing editor's office. Leona was sitting behind her sleek black desk, talking on the phone and gesticulating wildly. Elizabeth knocked quietly on the open door.

Leona looked up and smiled, holding up an index finger as a sign meaning, *Just one minute*. Then she waved Elizabeth in.

47

Elizabeth took a seat in the leather armchair across from Leona's desk, watching the managing editor in admiration. Leona was clearly agitated, but her voice was controlled and quietly authoritative. A tall, stylish woman with an aggressive management style and clear charisma, she was everything Elizabeth wanted to be someday.

Elizabeth had liked Leona from the start. From day one, her boss had been straightforward with her. She'd made it clear that she expected a lot of hard work from Elizabeth, including meeting tight deadlines and putting in long hours. But she'd made her feel at home as well. She'd told Elizabeth she considered them a team, and as a team, she wanted diligence, input, and honesty. "As long as we're both completely honest with each other, we should get along wonderfully," she had said. She had all the qualities Elizabeth admired—independence, drive, and integrity.

Leona drummed her pearl-colored French-cut nails on the desk top. "The deadline is this afternoon at two o'clock," she was saying. "I want the article here *then*, on my desk. Is that clear?" She listened for a minute, then smiled. "Of course, I know. Creativity can't be forced." Leona ran a finger through her dark blond hair. "Don't force it, dear. Just *push* it a little, OK?"

Leona hung up the phone and exhaled deeply, blowing a long blond lock out of her face. "Writers!" she said with a sigh. "They're quite a temperamental group." Leona shook her head. "Sometimes I think they're worse than models."

Then Leona clapped her hands brusquely and turned her attention to Elizabeth. "So, how are you?"

"I'm OK," Elizabeth said slowly. "But I'm afraid we won't be able to do our double date tonight, after all," she said. "It's all over between me and Todd." She blinked, willing herself not to cry in front of her boss. Elizabeth clenched her fingers together in her lap, praying that Leona wouldn't ask for details.

But Leona was all business. "Oh, it's just as well," she said, waving a dismissive hand. "Your career should come first anyway. You're too young to be tied down. Believe me, Elizabeth, if you want to succeed, you have to throw yourself body, mind, and soul into your work. Romance just gets in the way."

Elizabeth let out her breath, relieved at Leona's matter-of-fact tone. If she had been sympathetic, Elizabeth was sure she would have burst into tears.

Leona leaned back and crossed one long, lean leg over the other, bobbing a low-heeled black pump in the air. "Actually, I was going to have to cancel our date anyway," she said. "I have a feeling that Sam—my boyfriend—is going to pop the question tonight." She gave Elizabeth an intimate smile. "Obviously, we'd want to be alone for that."

Elizabeth looked at her in surprise. "But what about career first?" she asked.

49

Leona shrugged. "Some of us can do it all," she responded lightly.

Elizabeth looked down, feeling like a total failure. She wished she were more like her boss.

"Now, enough woman talk," Leona said, sitting up straight and brushing her hands together. "Let's talk business. I want to give you the rundown of the upcoming special edition. We worked out the details last night in a brainstorming session." Leona's hazel eyes gleamed. "Elizabeth, you're going to love this idea."

Elizabeth forced a smile, but she felt completely lethargic inside. At the moment, she couldn't care less about *Flair* magazine or fashion or professional success.

Leona held up a mock pasteup of the cover. It featured a model in front of some kind of ancient ruins, with the title *Antiquity Today*. "It's a Greek and Roman antiquity edition," Leona explained. "We're going to play with the idea of past and present—with special fashion exclusives on modern styles in ancient settings, the fashions of antiquity, and the past in the present."

Despite herself, Elizabeth's ears perked up. "Like the retro look," she said. "Only *really* retro."

"Exactly," Leona said with a smile. She picked up a note pad and scanned it. "The travel section will contain a layout on Mediterranean holidays," she continued, "and the issue will contain feature articles on ancient mythology and on the lives of

Greek and Roman women in ancient times, with an emphasis on social structures, women's issues, sexism, and so forth."

As Leona continued to explain the concept, Elizabeth began to get some of her enthusiasm back. A million ideas popped into her head for the new issue. She pictured an article entitled "The Goddess in You" covering the ancient mythological figures. She wondered what the quality of life was for women in ancient times and what their social roles had been. Her fingers itched to do a search on the Lexis/Nexis machine in the office. Lexis/Nexis was a dream source of information for journalists, providing access to articles from every major newspaper and magazine in the United States.

Leona snapped her notebook shut. "So what do you think?"

"Leona, it's a fabulous idea," Elizabeth breathed.

Leona smiled in satisfaction. "I knew you'd like it." She leaned in closer. "But this means a lot of work during the next week—fact checking, proof-reading, and some major research. And remember, the idea is highly confidential. We don't want anyone to know what the issue is about until it hits the newsstand."

Leona stood up, and Elizabeth took that as her cue to stand up too.

"I've written up a list of some of the things for

you to take care of today," Leona said, handing her a typed memo. "The most important task is research. I want you to search the Library of Congress and do a Lexis/Nexis run. By the end of the day, I want to know everything that's been printed on Greek and Roman antiquity in the last fifty years. And I mean *everything*."

"No problem," Elizabeth said, her chest tight with excitement. She headed back to her desk, filled with a new sense of determination. Leona was right. Relationships just got in the way. She was going to emulate Leona and throw herself into her work. After all, if she wanted to be successful in business, she couldn't let her personal life get her down.

Elizabeth sat down at her desk and flicked on her computer, ready to get to work.

Jessica paused on the top rung of a six-foot ladder in the main photography studio, surveying her work. For the past hour, she had been setting up for the morning's shoot. Nick Nolan, the set director, had come in early to prep her. It was a Greek Isles scene with a bright blue backdrop, huge white boulders, and a cascading waterfall.

Jessica gazed at the set in satisfaction. She had transformed the cool, airy studio into a hot Mediterranean paradise. The fake rocks cluttered together really looked like dusty white boulders, and they glinted against the backdrop as if against a blinding blue sky. Jessica had propped up the waterfall on the far left, but she wasn't quite sure how to hook up the mechanism.

She climbed all the way to the top of the ladder and carefully positioned the lights above the backdrop, trying to set them up just like Quentin wanted. Then she stepped down carefully and took a seat on the highest rung. She rubbed her shoulders and stretched out her neck. It was only ten A.M., and Jessica's back and shoulders were already aching from moving the fake rocks around and transporting huge buckets of water.

Where is everybody? Jessica wondered. Usually Quentin was there at the crack of dawn, barking out orders. And Simone normally didn't give Jessica a moment's peace, keeping her occupied with the most mundane tasks imaginable. *Maybe she won't show up,* Jessica thought hopefully. *Maybe one of her high heels got caught in a sewage drain and she twisted her ankle. Or maybe she slipped down the drain entirely.* Then Quentin would have no choice but to use Jessica in her place. With Simone out of the way, Jessica was sure she could get through to Quentin.

Suddenly the door swung open and Quentin breezed through, a camera slung over his shoulder. Jessica's tongue went dry. What if Quentin had forgotten all about the other day in the darkroom? What if he forgot about their date entirely? After all, you could never tell with artists. And

Quentin was a particularly temperamental one.

But Quentin whistled under his breath as he took in the set. "Hey, looks good," he said, smiling up at her. "A Greek paradise and a Greek goddess on her modern Mount Olympus." He sauntered over to her. "Want some help getting down from there?"

"Sure," Jessica said softly, standing up and turning around.

Jessica took a few steps down the ladder. Then Quentin put his strong arms around her waist and lifted her to the floor. His hands lingered on her waist as he turned her around to face him. "Looking forward to our dinner tonight?" he asked in a low voice.

"Of course," Jessica said coyly.

"You should be, because I'm taking you to the most exclusive restaurant in all of L.A.," he whispered in her ear. "It's called Chez Paul, and it's on Hollywood Boulevard. I'll meet you there at eight."

"Am I interrupting something?" came a saucy voice from behind them. Jessica and Quentin whirled around. It was Simone, a lazy catlike look of contentment on her cold features. Jessica bit her lip. It was a well-known fact at *Flair* that Simone and Quentin had been involved for some time. Jessica was thrilled to flaunt her flirtation with Quentin, but she wasn't sure he'd feel the same way.

But Quentin wasn't disturbed by Simone's arrival. "Simone, you're late," he said flatly.

Simone shrugged. "I needed my beauty sleep."

Quentin headed for the darkroom, suddenly all business. "Simone, go to wardrobe. Jessica, set up the lights. We'll be shooting in an hour."

Jessica pounced on Simone as soon as Quentin had disappeared into his cave of chemicals. "So, did you have fun with my sister's boyfriend last night?"

Simone was totally unperturbed by Jessica's attitude. "Todd's OK for a high-school boy," she responded. "He'll be good for a few photo ops, at least."

"Photo ops?" Jessica demanded. "Like what?"

Simone whipped out a copy of *Los Angeles Living* and held it up for Jessica to see. On the front page was a huge, tacky color photo of Todd in Simone's arms.

Jessica was speechless. This girl was too much. She was just glad that Elizabeth would never read a paper of such low quality. If she saw the photo, she'd really flip out.

"Now, if you'll excuse me," Simone purred, waltzing past her, "I've got to get dressed." She turned back before she entered the dressing room. "Oh, I'd like to try out a few pairs of shoes. Would you mind bringing me a half dozen pairs of Italian sandals from wardrobe?"

Jessica's eyes narrowed as she walked away to do the Twig's bidding. She was going to find a way to get Simone. If it was the last thing she did.

Chapter 4

Leona stopped in Elizabeth's office before lunch, a smooth black leather briefcase in her hand. "Elizabeth, I'll be in a brainstorming meeting for a few hours," she said. "That means I'll be indisposed. OK?"

"Sure, Leona," Elizabeth responded. "I'll field all your calls."

Leona turned back before she walked out the door. "I'm going to be pitching a few new ideas. Wish me luck." Then she winked and headed toward the elevator.

Elizabeth's heart began to pound. What did that wink mean? Did that mean that Leona was going to pitch *her* idea? When Elizabeth had first come up with the idea for an interactive monthly column, she was sure she had hit on something. She had done some research into other fashion magazines and found reader involvement to be both a popular trend and a good selling point for fashion magazines. She had been sure her idea would fly because it was interactive, but simple to implement. But when she approached Leona with the idea on Wednesday, the managing editor had been very discouraging, and Elizabeth had deflated like a popped balloon.

Elizabeth had been very disappointed at the time. But now she tapped the eraser end of a pencil on her Lexis/Nexis printout, deep in thought. Maybe Leona was taking her idea more seriously than she had realized.

Well, even if she weren't, Elizabeth resolved to push the idea. After all, journalists had to be aggressive. They had to pitch their ideas—and not take no for an answer. Her boss's pep talk this morning had done its job. Elizabeth was determined to make a name for herself, even if that meant putting herself on the line. She could already picture the column in the next issue—the theme would be women's advances from ancient times to the present and how fashion reflected that change.

Elizabeth turned back to the computer screen and typed in the last line on her report. Then she pressed "save" and "print." The document rolled out of the printer, and Elizabeth pulled it out with a flourish, looking at it with satisfaction. It was only noon, and she had already completed her research.

Not only had she printed out a list of all the articles published in the United States on the topic of women in antiquity in the last fifty years, but she had written up a small report with article titles and summaries as well. Elizabeth was sure Leona was going to be impressed. Slinging her blazer over her arm, Elizabeth tucked the collection of articles into a file folder. Then she stopped in Leona's office and dropped her work on the desk.

On her way to the elevator, Elizabeth peeked into Reggie's office. Reggie was sitting behind her desk, almost hidden behind an enormous pile of papers, photographs and magazine layouts.

"Feel like getting some lunch?" Elizabeth asked.

Reggie shook her head ruefully, pointing to a half-eaten sandwich laying on a blueprint. "It's going to be another long day," she said with a sigh.

"Well, let me know if you need any help," Elizabeth offered.

"Thanks, Liz," Reggie said. Then she cocked her head and studied Elizabeth. "Hey, you look much better. Did something happen that I should know about?"

Elizabeth shrugged. "No, nothing at all." Then she smiled. "Who needs men, anyway?" she asked.

Reggie grinned, giving her a thumbs-up signal.

Elizabeth hummed as she headed for the elevator bank, feeling pleased with herself. She checked out her appearance in the mirrored elevator doors as she waited. Her hair was a bit wild, and she combed it into place with her fingers, admiring the snazzy, shoulder-length cut with longer pieces in front. She looked every bit the young professional. She was wearing a short, light green dress and black pumps with green-colored toes. Though the color was somewhat daring, it suited her, bringing out her rosy-colored complexion and the golden highlights in her hair. Elizabeth smoothed down her skirt and put on her long blazer, shifting from one foot to the other as she waited.

Finally, the doors opened and Elizabeth stepped in gracefully.

"Hey, great color," said a woman in the elevator with burnt amber–colored hair. "Is that a Bartucci design?"

Elizabeth smiled. "Actually, it's one of Bibi's latest—she's an unknown designer," she said. She chuckled inwardly at her own words. Bibi's wasn't exactly a designer, but rather a store at the Sweet Valley Mall.

The woman nodded. "Up-and-coming fashions are really the way to go. Unknowns are often one step ahead of the rest."

As she headed down the hall to the cafeteria, Elizabeth felt halfway decent for the first time since she had seen Todd kissing Simone. She had thrown herself into her work that morning and was proud of herself for being able to concentrate. Not only had she had a productive, professional morning, but she looked the part of a young executive as well. Leona was right—she didn't need a boyfriend. She could make it all on her own.

Elizabeth held her head high as she walked by the newsstand in the lobby. Then she gasped out loud and did a double take. A copy of *Los Angeles Living* was displayed right in the middle of the newsstand, with a horrendously garish photo of Todd in Simone's arms.

"Supermodel Simone and playboy Todd Wilkins danced till dawn," the bold caption read.

Elizabeth's throat constricted, and she took a few steps back. She felt as though she had been whacked in the chest with a ten-ton stack of magazines. Tears of anger and frustration sprang to her eyes. Breaking her heart wasn't enough. Now Todd had to *humiliate* her as well.

"Wow, nice job, Jessica," Shelly Fabian said to Jessica in the photography studio at lunchtime. Shelly was the makeup artist and had become Jessica's friend. She was a warm woman with smooth ebony skin and ample hips. She cocked her head to the left, the colorful glass beads at the end of her long, skinny braids tinkling lightly. "You've really captured the look of the Mediterranean."

Jessica rubbed her dirty hands on her tangerine-colored miniskirt, eyeing the set wearily. "I should hope so," she said. "Because I've spent about four hours putting this together."

The set was all ready for the Greek Isles shoot. One of the set designers had helped Jessica connect the mechanism for the waterfall, and it was set up to drip down the rocks. Now Simone the Stick just had to jut her bony hips into the scene.

Jessica swiped her hair out of her eyes and smacked her hands together, sending bits of blue chalk into the air. She blinked, looking in dismay as bits of the blue backdrop landed all over her new pale orange skirt. She didn't know why she bothered getting dressed up for work anymore. By the time she got home, she looked like a rag. Her cream-colored blouse was already stained and wrinkled, and her skirt was smudged with dirt.

Jessica took a seat on one of the extra fake rocks on the corner, slipping off her high-heeled pumps and massaging her toes. Then she closed her eyes and leaned her head against the wall, wishing for two basic things: food and sleep. She was dirty and exhausted from spending the morning at the Stick's beck and call. Plus, she hadn't eaten anything at all that day, and sharp hunger pains were shooting through her stomach.

Just then Simone emerged from the dressing room. "What's wrong?" she asked Jessica in a haughty voice. "Can't handle the pace of the fashion world?"

"No, I can't handle the *face* of the fashion world," Jessica retorted.

"Very cute. You made a pun," Simone said

tightly, strutting across the room. She was wearing a body-hugging, floor-length blue silk halter dress with an oval hole cut out over the midriff. Her blue eyes were piercing, and her skin was paler than ever in the dress. She was supposed to be a Greek goddess, but she looked more like an ice princess. Or an ice *witch*.

Simone struck a pose, jutting one hip forward. "What in the world is Quentin doing?" she complained, rubbing her forehead with her right hand.

"Hey, watch it honey," Shelly said quickly. "This face of the fashion world is mine. I spent an hour on your makeup this morning, and I don't want you ruining my creation."

"Sorry," Simone scowled, dropping her hand quickly. She crossed her long legs, waiting impatiently. Then she stood back and studied the scene, her cold blue eyes squinting.

"Jessica, I think that rock is off," Simone said, pointing to the large white boulder in the center. "It should be further to the left."

Jessica rolled her eyes. Simone had no idea where anything belonged on the set. But she slipped her pumps back on and stood up. She hobbled onto the set and kneeled down to pick up the fake rock.

Suddenly the waterfall rushed on. "*Wha—?*" Jessica sputtered as water crashed over her, drenching her hair and clothes.

"Oh, *sorry* about that," Simone said. She had

stepped on the lever controlling the water supply. "I didn't realize you were in the way."

Jessica flung her wet hair back, splattering droplets of water all over Simone's silk dress. Shelly tried not to grin as she handed Jessica a white towel.

Simone gasped and took in the splattered dress in alarm. "Look what you've done! You've ruined my outfit!"

"Oh, *sorry* about that," Jessica said, echoing Simone. "I didn't realize you were in the way." She rubbed the towel briskly through her hair.

"Well, you're going to have to go to wardrobe and fetch me another one," Simone demanded, gazing at the stains on the dress in dismay. "This is an original Rafael Bartucci design. I don't think Quentin is going to be too happy when he sees what you've done." She sent Jessica a withering glance. "In fact, he'll probably fire you on the spot."

Jessica shrugged. "I'll just explain to him that it was all a mistake—that you didn't mean to turn on the waterfall." She stepped out of a low-heeled pump and turned it upside down, dumping water on the ground.

Simone sputtered angrily. "How dare you accuse me—"

"Hey, what's going on here?" Quentin suddenly asked in his deep voice.

Simone and Jessica both turned and started speaking at once.

"Jessica ruined my dress!" Simone shrieked.

"Simone turned on the water!" Jessica exclaimed at the same time.

"Simone needs to change," Shelly explained.

Quentin raised a hand in the air. "OK, everybody take a break and get cleaned up. We'll do the shoot after lunch." He turned back to the darkroom shaking his head. "Women," he muttered.

Shelly leaned in close to Jessica. "Models," she said.

Jessica giggled, giving Simone a sugary sweet smile. "See you after lunch!" she said, then she waltzed toward the elevator. She didn't even care about the fact that her hair was plastered to her head and her outfit was damp. It was worth it just to see Simone sputter.

The elevator bank opened and a cute young delivery boy with straight brown hair came out. Jessica smiled at him and stepped in.

"Are you Jessica Wakefield?" he asked.

"The same," Jessica nodded.

"I've got a delivery for you," he said. Jessica stepped back out quickly, and the guy handed her a package. "This was sent to you anonymously." Then he winked and got back in the elevator.

Jessica looked at the brown package curiously, holding it up to her ear and shaking it. It didn't move, but it smelled delicious. Smiling, Jessica quickly ripped open the envelope and pulled out a plastic dish. Then she lifted the cover off the platter.

It was an elaborate plate of colorful sushi. Jessica's stomach growled hungrily, and she smiled. Quentin had really outdone himself. She was impressed. And she was looking forward to their date tonight.

But as she sat down on the rock in the corner, a disturbing thought struck her. She had almost forgotten about her date with Cameron tonight, a date that she was looking forward to as well— maybe even more so. Jessica dipped a piece of sushi into teriyaki sauce, pondering what she'd do about the fact that she had to be in two places at once. . . .

"Life as Humiliation," Elizabeth said out loud to the computer screen, typing in titles for her teenage autobiography in her office after lunch. "I Was Ditched for a Supermodel." "From Bad to Worse." She lifted a forkful of salad to her mouth and forced herself to chew and swallow.

After having seen the incriminating photo of Todd and Simone, Elizabeth had been too upset to show her face in public. She had bought a salad from the salad bar and had taken it up to her office to eat. But the food was just making her nauseated. Elizabeth pushed away her half eaten plate, staring dejectedly at the titles on the screen.

Elizabeth heard Leona return to her office and sunk lower in her seat. *Time to face the music,* she thought, preparing herself for the worst. She braced herself mentally and pulled herself out of the chair. After seeing Todd's picture, Elizabeth felt immune to other pain. Even if Leona told her the entire editorial board hated her idea, Elizabeth wouldn't feel worse than she already did.

Still, her heart pounded as she knocked on Leona's door.

"Yes," Leona called out.

Elizabeth popped her head in. "Hi—I," she said, stuttering slightly. She took a deep breath and tried to sound casual. "I just wanted to know if you by any chance ran my idea by the editorial board."

"Oh, yes, your little idea," Leona said. "As a matter of fact, I did." She gestured to the chair across from her desk. "Why don't you come in?"

Little idea? Elizabeth felt her face flush as she slid into the leather chair.

"Well, I'm sorry to tell you this, Elizabeth, but the board rejected the idea."

Elizabeth swallowed and nodded. *From Bad to Worse,* she thought. *Definitely.*

"Now, don't take it badly, dear," Leona said. "The material was very well written, but unfortunately, the idea wasn't terribly original. The reader-writer concept has been tossed around editorial for years. We've discovered that kind of thing just isn't viable."

"Not—not viable," Elizabeth stuttered, flushing as she heard herself repeating Leona's words like an idiot.

"Yes, you see, when readers write our material,

the quality of writing goes way down. And quality of writing is what makes *Flair* stand out from other fashion magazines."

"I see," Elizabeth said, nodding and blinking back tears. She was wrong when she thought she couldn't feel worse. Because she could—and she did. One rejection on top of another was just too much. Even worse than her words was the look in Leona's eyes—it was a mixture of pity and disappointment.

Leona gave Elizabeth a condescending smile. "Keep trying, Elizabeth," she said. "You've got potential. I'm sure you'll come up with something one of these days."

Elizabeth was crushed. She scraped back her chair and stood up quickly.

"Oh, and can you proof these notes?" Leona asked, handing her a huge stack of yellow memo paper.

Elizabeth bit her lip. "Sure," she said, slinking out of the office.

Chapter 5

"Stupid," Todd muttered, glancing at his reflection critically in the rearview mirror as he switched lanes on the highway. "Stupid, stupid, stupid." Todd was on his way to *Flair* for a late afternoon photo shoot. It was only one P.M., but he wanted to get to the office early to try to make up with Elizabeth. He was hoping to get to her before she heard about the photo on the cover of *Los Angeles Living*.

As he sped along the Santa Monica Freeway in his black BMW, Todd berated himself for having been so thoughtless the day before. He really had let this modeling thing get to his head. He was just so flattered by Simone's attention that he hadn't resisted her kiss—or her invitation to go to one of the hottest nightclubs in L.A.

But Todd knew that Elizabeth was the one he

really loved. To be honest, even when he had been with Simone, all he could think about was Elizabeth.

Todd screeched into the parking lot of the Mode building, a modern high-rise that housed *Flair* and the other magazines in the Mode group. He jumped out of his car quickly, anxious to talk to his girlfriend. He really hoped she'd understand. And forgive him. Of course, even if she accepted his apology, he wouldn't be able to go out with her anyway. He was grounded. For a month.

A whole month, Todd thought, scowling as he crossed the marble floor of the glamorous lobby. He couldn't believe how unfair his parents were being. So he went out to a nightclub and stayed out late. Big deal. He was almost an adult. There was no reason his life should be completely limited by his parents' dumb rules.

But at the moment, being grounded wasn't the problem. Elizabeth was. Todd bit his lip. He knew how stubborn Elizabeth could be when she was hurt. Or when her pride was wounded. Todd leaned against the wall in the lobby, wondering how he could get her back.

Then he was struck with an idea—*flowers.* Elizabeth loved flowers. He would buy her a beautiful bouquet, and when she caught sight of his repenting face and his flower-laden arms, she wouldn't be able to resist him. Todd quickly headed for the florist on the ground floor.

A few minutes later, Todd stood in front of the elevator, a dozen long-stemmed red roses in his arms. Whistling to himself, he punched the button. The elevator door wheezed open, and the cloying scent of perfume greeted him as he stepped in. All around him stood nearly identical leggy women in short skirts and long blazers.

"Looks like some lucky girl is going to be pretty happy," a sophisticated-looking brunette next to him said.

Todd gave her a half smile, hoping she was right. The elevator stopped at every floor, and Todd impatiently shifted his weight from one foot to the other. He pulled a pen out of his pocket and scribbled a quick note on the card stuck in the bouquet. "Please forgive me, Liz. I love you forever—Todd."

He tucked the card back into the flowers and looked up at the lighted numbers at the top of the elevator. He blinked as he realized they were already on the eleventh floor and the doors were about to close. Sticking an arm out, he caught the door and pushed it open. A few impatient sighs came from the women. Todd grimaced apologetically and pushed his way out.

Without glancing at the receptionist, he hurried down the hall to the editorial department. Taking a deep breath, he knocked sharply on the door to Elizabeth's office. But there was no response. Feeling nervous, he rapped again. Nothing. Todd pushed the door open slowly and peeked his head in. "Liz?" he asked. But her chair was empty.

Todd sighed and headed back to the main desk. "Excuse me," he said to the receptionist, a young woman with glossy auburn hair and horn-rimmed black glasses. "Do you know where Elizabeth Wakefield is?"

The receptionist pushed up her glasses, glancing down at a list in front of her. "I believe she's in Leona Peirson's office at the moment."

A wave of disappointment washed over him. Todd hesitated, wondering what to do. He could leave the flowers with the receptionist, but he didn't want to leave without seeing Elizabeth. He needed to work things out with her—*immediately*. There was no way he'd get through his photo shoot with Simone if he didn't resolve things with Elizabeth.

Todd cleared his throat nervously. "Could you please buzz the office and tell her I'm here?"

The receptionist lifted a sharply arched eyebrow. "Is she expecting you?" she asked.

Todd nodded, his face flushing.

"And who shall I say is calling?" she asked sharply.

"Todd," he said, trying to sound authoritative. "Todd Wilkins."

"Next category: feature articles," Leona said, pacing across the wine-colored carpet that lined

71

the floor of her sleek office. "'Greek Island Getaways,' 'Roman Empires,' 'Empresses,' and 'Sexism in Athens.'"

Elizabeth quickly scratched down Leona's words on a yellow legal pad, trying desperately to keep up with her boss.

Leona paused. "Did you get all that?"

Elizabeth nodded and repeated her words back to her. Dropping her pen on the pad, she stretched out her aching fingers. She was taking dictation from Leona for the layout of the upcoming Greek and Roman antiquity edition. Leona had been dictating nonstop for about an hour, and her words came faster than Elizabeth could record them.

Leona put a hand on a slender hip, her eyes narrowed in thought. "OK, great. Now, where were we?"

Elizabeth scanned her notes. "We're up to fashion exclusives."

Leona nodded. "Right, right. Fashion. Let's see. Make these bullets, OK?"

Elizabeth frowned. "Bullets?" she inquired.

"Put it in outline form," Leona explained quickly, a hint of irritation in her voice.

Elizabeth nodded and hunched over her pad, readying herself for the next barrage of words.

"First fashion spread—'Back to the Future'—the return of metallics in Rafael Bartucci designs, modern cuts, and fabrics. Second spread—'Retro-active'—that's with a hyphen—the retro look in forties and seventies designs. Third spread—'Lingering Luxuries'—the Lina Lapin faux-fur fall line and—"

The intercom crackled, and Leona stopped midsentence. Sighing, she pressed the button for the intercom. "Yes?" she asked, tapping a low heel impatiently.

"A Mr. Todd Wilkins is here to see Elizabeth Wakefield," Anne, the receptionist, announced.

Elizabeth's eyes almost popped out of her head. She couldn't believe Todd's gall. How *dare* he interrupt her in the managing editor's office! Elizabeth's face flamed in anger and embarrassment. Todd's ego was obviously getting way too big for his boy toy's body.

Leona pursed her lips together and gave Elizabeth a sharp look.

Elizabeth swallowed hard. "Sorry, Leona," she said softly. "This will just take a second." Then she leaned over the intercom on the desk and pressed the button.

Todd paced back and forth in the crowded receptionist area, his stomach twisting in anticipation. Since he had been waiting, the room had filled up with people. It seemed as though half of the editors in the department had after-lunch meetings scheduled. Chic, well-dressed models and suave literary types with manuscripts in their hands spoke in hushed voices in the waiting area, and a number of distinguished-looking men in suits were conversing in the corner.

Todd fluffed out his flowers and sat down in a chair, drumming his fingers on the arm of the chair.

Suddenly the intercom crackled and Todd stood up, waiting to be called into the office. He breathed a sigh of relief as he recognized Elizabeth's voice over the intercom. Her voice came through strong and clear, and everybody quieted down to listen. "This is Elizabeth Wakefield," she said. "Please inform Mr. Wilkins that I never want to see him again."

Mortified, Todd grabbed onto the arm of the chair for support.

The receptionist looked straight at him, barely suppressing a smile. "Uh, Mr. Wilkins, did you get that?"

Todd nodded quickly, his face flushing with embarrassment as everybody in the office turned to look at him. He swallowed hard, feeling his face grow prickly hot. For a moment, Todd stood paralyzed, wishing only that the floor would open up and he would fall through to the first floor. Then he became aware of the stares and whispers. A few people even giggled and pointed.

Feeling more humiliated than he had in his whole life, Todd grabbed his flowers and slouched out of the office. Trying to retain some dignity, he controlled his speed as he beat a path down the hall.

But as he punched the button at the elevator

bank, his embarrassment turned to anger. He couldn't believe Elizabeth wouldn't even hear him out. And he couldn't believe she would publicly humiliate him like that. He angrily bent the roses in half and threw them in a trash can, pricking his fingers as he did so. Then he tore up the card he had written, smearing it with blood. Oblivious to the pain in his fingers, he threw the blood-stained pieces into the trash and stepped into the elevator.

Fine, he thought, hitting the button for the art department on the ninth floor. *Elizabeth can have it her way. I'll never speak to her again!*

"Jessica, do you think you could run down to the mail room to pick up a package for me?" Quentin asked, blinking in the light as he came out of the darkroom after lunch. "I'd like to take a look at the proofs before we start this afternoon's shoot." His shaggy blond hair was more disheveled than usual, and he had a distracted air about him.

"Sure," Jessica agreed. She was just finishing up her lunch. She popped the last bit of sushi into her mouth and stuffed the empty container back into the brown envelope. She stood up and threw the bag into a nearby trash receptacle. "Thanks for lunch," she said, flashing the famous photographer a winning Wakefield smile.

"No problem," Quentin responded. "All of *Flair's* employees get a full hour."

Jessica frowned, trying to work out his puzzling

response. Then she shrugged. *Oh well,* she thought. *He's an artist. Artists are eccentric.*

As she headed to the mail room, though, her thoughts turned from Quentin to Cameron. Jessica had decided over lunch that she was going to have to cancel her date with Cameron, and she wasn't looking forward to it.

Jessica bit her lip as she headed for the mail room behind the first floor lobby. Now Cameron was never going to trust her. If he found out she was canceling their date to go out with Quentin, he'd never speak to her again. It would only confirm his worst thoughts.

Jessica sighed as she walked through the cluttered storage nooks and sorting areas of the mail room. Cameron was wrong about her. She *didn't* care at all about people with money or success. She did care about her *own* success, however, and Quentin was the only one who could help her with that. But Cameron would never understand.

Jessica caught sight of Cameron packing boxes in the back. Her heart skipped a beat at the sight of him, and she hid behind a loading dock to watch him for a moment. Cameron was about nineteen or twenty years old, with a strong build, curly brown hair, and big brown eyes. Today he looked particularly cute in faded jeans and a button-down denim shirt with the sleeves rolled up. He was lifting boxes and throwing them in piles, his biceps bulging with each movement. Jessica sucked in her breath. It was like watching a coiled animal in motion.

Not for the first time, she wished *he* were the guy who could help her further her career as a model—and not Quentin. Taking a deep breath, she stepped around the dock and cleared her throat.

Cameron turned and smiled. The sight of his deep brown eyes crinkling at the corners sent sparks down her spine.

"Doing some housecleaning?" Jessica asked with a smile.

Cameron nodded. "Exactly," he said. He heaved a few more boxes onto the loading dock, arm muscles rippling. Jessica felt a bit mesmerized. "I was feeling a little boxed in," he added with a grin.

Then his eyes widened as he took in her damp clothes and hair. "What happened?" he teased. "Was there a thunderstorm in the art department this morning?"

"Something like that," Jessica admitted, jumping up on a rickety old wooden desk in the corner. "I had an encounter with the Fashion Witch." Jessica had already given Cameron the full details of her difficult work situation. Now she quickly recounted the morning's events to him.

Cameron laughed and shook his head when she finished. "The famous Simone shows her claws again." He came up close to Jessica and wrapped his arms around her, rubbing her back briskly. "Am I warming you up?"' he whispered in her ear.

Heating me up is more like it, Jessica thought. Her whole body felt as if it were on fire. Unable to resist, she leaned back and lifted her face for a kiss. At the feel of Cameron's warm lips on hers, electricity cascaded down her whole body.

Then she pulled back abruptly, remembering that she had come down to cancel her date with Cameron, not to kiss him. "Uh, I'd better get back," she said. "Quentin sent me down for a package."

Cameron threw a box aside and reached for a package on the desk marked Photographs. "I know," he said, handing her the big brown envelope. "I've been expecting you." Then he glanced at his watch. "You're only a half hour late."

"Punctuality is not one of my best qualities," Jessica said. She took the package from him and laid it on the desk next to her.

"Oh? What are your best qualities?" Cameron asked, a sparkle in his beautiful brown eyes.

"Hmm, let's see," Jessica said, ticking them off on her fingers. "Beauty, talent, joie de vivre—"

"And modesty," Cameron interrupted.

Jessica lowered her head and batted her eyebrows, making Cameron laugh.

"So, are you excited about our date tonight?" he asked.

Jessica opened her mouth to say no, but found herself saying yes.

Then she hopped off the desk and picked up the package, wondering what she was getting herself into. "You might be surprised by what a date with me is like," she warned. "Some people have even told me that I have enough personality for two people. . . ."

Cameron winked. "I think I can handle it," he said. "What time should I pick you up?"

"Oh, you don't have to drive all the way out to Sweet Valley," Jessica said quickly. "Why don't we just meet at the restaurant?"

Cameron shrugged. "As you like. What did you have in mind?"

Jessica swallowed hard. "Um, I've always wanted to try out that French restaurant on Hollywood Boulevard—Chez Paul."

Cameron whistled softly, looking surprised. "Chez Paul," he repeated. "That's quite a choice."

"Is that OK with you?" Jessica asked worriedly.

"Of course," Cameron responded. "I love French food."

Jessica grimaced, concerned about Quentin's exotic choice. Maybe the famous photographer could eat out in style every night, but Cameron couldn't possibly afford a chic French restaurant. Jessica sighed inwardly. In any case, it was too late now. "How about eight-thirty?" she asked.

"Sounds perfect," Cameron agreed. Then he waggled a teasing finger at her. "Try to be on time tonight."

"I'll try," Jessica responded. "But I never wear a watch."

Cameron pulled her close for a last kiss. "You're worth waiting for," he said, his voice low and husky. Jessica shivered in pleasure as the heat of his body enveloped her. She found herself wishing for the thousandth time since they'd met that he wasn't merely a mail-room worker, that he was the one who could help her career instead of Quentin. . . . And then she forgot her wishes, lost in the hot passion of his kiss.

Chapter 6

"Lean your head way back, Todd," Michael Rietz, the stylist, directed on Friday afternoon.

Todd slid down obediently in the chair and hung his head backward, shifting impatiently as Michael teased a comb through his wavy brown hair. Todd had spent an hour in wardrobe and now he was in Michael's salon having his hair done for the upcoming Roman Empire shoot. He was outfitted in a white toga with gold trim around the neckline, and his feet were bare. Todd was supposed to look like Roman royalty, but instead he felt like some kind of fashion slave.

Michael eyed the array of styling gels and mousses on the counter, selecting a few bottles and setting them aside. Then he picked up a pair of scissors and began snipping expertly at the ends of Todd's hair.

"You're not going to cut it all off, are you?" Todd asked worriedly.

"Shh," Michael rebuked him lightly. "The artist is at work."

The well-known hair stylist took a step back and cocked his head, studying his creation through narrowed eyes. Then he nodded and picked up a bottle of gel. A young man with long, straight dark hair, Michael had a wry sense of humor. Even though he didn't seem to take anyone in the department seriously, he certainly took his *job* seriously.

Michael squeezed some gel onto his palm and massaged it deftly through Todd's hair. Then he slicked Todd's hair back and tucked the ends under, securing them firmly with bobby pins in the back.

"Close your eyes, Todd," Michael warned, lifting an ominous aerosol can in the air.

Todd squeezed his eyes shut, scrunching his nose as Michael spritzed his hair with the artificial-smelling fumes.

"OK, you can look now," Michael said.

Todd opened his eyes warily.

"Voilà!" Michael exclaimed with a wave of his hand.

Todd stared at his image in the mirror in horror. Michael had transformed his hair into a tiny cap on his head. Todd patted his head quickly. It felt hard and crusty. He turned his head quickly from left to right. Not a hair moved. "But—but it's a *hat!*" Todd sputtered, patting his head again.

Michael grinned. "Exactly! Now you look the part of Mark Anthony." He whipped off the towel from Todd's shoulders and whisked his neck with a brush.

"You're done?" Todd gasped in alarm.

Michael shook his head, a small smile on his face. "Don't worry, Todd. It'll look fantastic in the shoot. You'll see. You just need the proper lights and the proper camera."

Todd exhaled sharply. "OK, I hope you're right."

Todd stood up and wrapped his toga tightly around him. He took a deep breath as he headed out the door, feeling particularly naked with his flat hair and nothing but a sheet around him.

When Todd returned to the main studio, the place was bustling with activity. Quentin was conferring with the set director in the corner. A number of lighting specialists were scattered about the room, adjusting tall bluish lights in the corners. Shelly was setting up a makeup table covered with a vast array of tubes and jars of cosmetics. And a few assistants were carrying props and ladders across the room.

Even though everybody was running around, the set looked as though it was finished. A sparkling Roman Empire had been constructed, with a rich, gold palace flanked by two tall, pink marble columns. Todd had to admit that Jessica had done a good job. In fact, she even seemed to have a talent for set design. Todd blinked as Jessica materialized before him. She was kneeling on the ground, unrolling a long red carpet along the floor. He hadn't even noticed her. With her golden-blond hair and her pale paint-splattered outfit, she blended right in with the set.

"OK, everybody, I'm ready," Simone announced in a breathy voice, waltzing out of the dressing room. Todd sucked in his breath at the sight of her. Simone was dressed up as Cleopatra, and she looked stunningly beautiful. She was draped in a long shimmering dress of gold lamé that was slit all the way up the leg. Her black hair hung straight at her chin, with false bangs cut across her forehead. Her china blue eyes slanted upward and her lips glowed a deep ruby red, offsetting the luminescent pearl of her face.

Simone felt Todd's eyes on her and struck a pose for him, resting a hand on her hip. "I like the outfit, Todd," she said appreciatively, gazing up and down his barely dressed body. Todd could feel his cheeks burning, and he clenched his jaw, resisting the impulse to flee back into the dressing room.

"I like it too," Jessica said with a snort from the set, where she had been listening to the exchange. She stood up and wiped her hands on her dress, adding flecks of red carpet to her yellow paint stains. "You look *great* in a dress, Todd." Disgust was plain in her voice.

"A lot better than *you,* I must say," Simone shot back, looking down at Jessica over her imperial nose.

"Some of us don't just have to *stand* for a living," Jessica retorted.

"Well, some of us—" Simone began.

Quentin clapped his hands together. "Places everybody!"

"Humph," Simone pouted, annoyed at being cut off. "Let's go, Todd," she said, taking his hand and leading him up the majestic red carpet onto the set. Todd pulled his hand out of her grasp, beginning to feel like kept property. It seemed as though Simone was bent on using him to make Quentin jealous and Jessica mad.

Quentin approached an elaborate camera mounted on a tripod and adjusted the lens. "OK, I want both of you in front of the column on the right," he instructed, joining them on the set. He positioned Simone with her hip jutting out and Todd standing right behind her, his hand on her hip.

Quentin took his place behind the camera and peered through the lens.

Todd stood perfectly still, holding the pose. But his whole body felt uncomfortable under the white-hot lights. His face was tight and heavy from the caked-on makeup, his cheek was twitching, and his hair-cap itched.

"Shelly, can you do a touch up on Todd?" Quentin asked. "I'm getting a glare on his face."

"I think that's coming from me," Jessica muttered under her breath.

Todd winced, but he didn't bother responding. The Wakefield twins were highly protective of each other, and he knew Jessica was furious at him for hurting Elizabeth. Todd sighed. He really couldn't blame her.

Shelly ran onto the set with a cosmetic brush in hand and quickly dusted Todd's face. Todd closed his eyes as she powdered, unsure of how much more of this he could endure. Now he could see why Elizabeth didn't wear much makeup. He didn't know how girls could stand spending so much time fussing with their face and hair.

Quentin peered through the lens again. "Great!" he breathed. "Don't move!" He quickly took the shot.

"Todd, shift behind Simone and put both your arms around her waist," Quentin directed. The camera clicked again.

"OK, Simone, I want a sultry look. Todd, give me that all-American smile," Quentin said, snapping the camera all the while as he spoke. "Simone, turn your eyes left, to the distance; Todd, follow suit." *Click* went the camera. "Terrific, Todd, you're a natural!" Quentin exclaimed. "You've really got talent!"

Too bad Elizabeth doesn't realize that, Todd

thought. *She doesn't know what she's losing.* Simone moved her body closer to his, and Quentin zoomed in for a close-up. Todd looked straight at the camera, defiance in his eyes. *She's probably just jealous. She just can't handle* me *being in the limelight for a change.*

With each click of the camera, Todd got angrier and angrier, thinking of how unfair Elizabeth was being. Sure, Elizabeth had a right to be mad at him, but this was between the two of them. He couldn't believe she had embarrassed him publicly. The more steamed he got, the closer he moved to Simone.

"Turn and face each other," Quentin directed. "Simone, look up into Todd's eyes. Give me your profile, honey."

Simone gazed up at him with laser blue eyes, the intensity of her stare causing him to catch his breath. Suddenly she leaned in close and kissed him. *Click* went the camera. "Fabulous!" Quentin exclaimed. "Hold that pose!"

Simone increased the pressure of his lips, and Todd stood perfectly still, horrified. He forced himself to respond to the kiss, wishing the moment would end.

Out of the corner of his eye, Todd saw Jessica storm out of the room. He pulled back from Simone, wincing. Jessica was sure to report everything to Elizabeth—from his outfit to his actions. Now Elizabeth would *really* never forgive him.

Then Todd shrugged. What was he worried about? He and Elizabeth weren't speaking anyway.

"Great! That's a wrap!" Quentin said excitedly, rewinding the film. "This roll is going to sizzle!"

Simone stretched out her long body lazily, causing the body-hugging fabric to reveal every contour of her body. Todd looked quickly at the ground, but not before Simone caught his eyes on her.

"So, would you like to go to another club tonight?" Simone asked in a husky voice. "There's a great place on Rodeo Drive called Inside Out. It's very in."

Todd scuffed his bare feet on the ground. "Well, actually, I'm grounded."

Simone lifted a thin, imperial eyebrow. "Grounded?" she asked, as if the word were distasteful to her.

Todd felt a flush heat up his cheeks. "Yeah, my parents saw the photo of us in that tabloid—and well—" He shrugged, feeling like an idiot.

Simone scoffed. "So blow them off," she said. "You're an adult, aren't you?"

"Well, uh —" Todd stuttered.

"Oh, come on, Todd," Simone sneered. "What are you, a man or a mouse?"

Simone's remarks hit home. *She's right,* Todd decided. He was earning big bucks now. He deserved to live his own life. He swallowed hard and tried to sound more self-assured than he felt. "I didn't say I was going to listen to them. What time should I pick you up?"

"Eleven-thirty sharp," Simone responded, pivoting on a high Rafael Bartucci heel.

Todd watched her long frame glide away, and he bit his lip worriedly. How had he gotten himself talked into this? *Well,* he decided, *I'm not entirely crazy.* He'd sneak out after his parents went to bed.

"You should have *seen* Todd and Simone at the photo shoot this afternoon," an outraged Jessica told Elizabeth as she steered the Jeep down the Santa Monica freeway after work. "It was *so-oo* disgusting."

Elizabeth closed her eyes and leaned back against the headrest. She didn't think she could bear to hear any more bad news.

"Todd was wearing—get this—a sheet—or a *dress* rather, and Simone was in a glued-on gold lamé number," Jessica reported.

A searing white-hot flash of jealousy shot through Elizabeth.

"And her dress wasn't the only thing glued onto her," Jessica continued. "The heat coming from Todd and Simone was hotter than Quentin's lights. They got closer and closer, and then they starting kissing. Can you believe it? And Quentin didn't even ask them to. They were practically making out on the set. I'm telling you—it was totally gross. If you ask me —"

But Elizabeth held up a hand. "Jessica, I didn't ask you."

"What?" Jessica asked, looking at her sister quickly.

"Look, I've heard enough, OK?" Elizabeth said sharply.

Jessica looked wounded. "I was just trying to protect you," she told her twin, a defensive note in her voice.

Elizabeth's voice softened. "Sorry, I didn't mean to jump on you like that. It's just that I've had it up to here with this Todd and Simone story." She held up a hand forehead high.

Jessica nodded and flipped on the radio, turning the knob to her favorite rock station. "OK," she said, "let's talk about something cheerier—like our weekend plans."

Elizabeth sighed. "I don't have any plans."

"You don't?" Jessica asked brightly. "So . . . what are you doing tonight?"

Elizabeth looked at her sister quickly, wondering what kind of plan she was hatching. But Jessica kept her eyes glued on the road, and so Elizabeth shrugged. "I'm planning to crawl under my covers and stay there until it's time to go to work on Monday. Or maybe I'll stay under there for the rest of my life."

"You know, Elizabeth, you should really go out and have fun," Jessica said, cutting her speed and turning off onto the exit ramp. "Staying home and moping isn't going to help at all. Besides, boring-as-butter Todd Wilkins isn't worth it."

Elizabeth looked at her twin suspiciously. Her

face looked innocent enough, but Elizabeth recognized a gleam in her twin's eyes.

"Do you have something in mind?" Elizabeth asked in an ironic tone.

"As a matter of fact, I do," Jessica replied. She turned her suddenly anguished face to her sister. "Elizabeth, you won't *believe* the situation I'm in!" she wailed.

"Try me," Elizabeth said dryly.

Jessica explained her sticky date situation in vivid detail, from Cameron's first kiss to his last one, and from Quentin's initial brush-off to his recent interest in her.

"So what's the problem?" Elizabeth asked when Jessica had finished. "You've got to cancel one of your dates, since you can't possibly be in two places at once."

Jessica pulled to a stop at an intersection and bit her lip. "But, Liz, I can't cancel *either* of them!" she whimpered. She stared straight ahead, blinking rapidly—and obviously trying to make her eyes fill with tears.

Elizabeth rolled her eyes at Jessica's pathetic attempt to get sympathy.

The light turned green, and Jessica stepped on the gas. "This is my big chance with Quentin," she explained. "We're going to discuss my future as a model. It's now or never."

Elizabeth nodded her head. "Yep, you can't cancel that one."

"And if I blow Cameron off, he'll never speak to me again! He's sure to find out about my date with Quentin." Jessica held her hands dramatically to her heart. "Elizabeth, Cameron could be the *one*."

Elizabeth groaned at her twin's overly dramatic performance. "Jess, keep your hands on the wheel."

Jessica grabbed the wheel with her right hand and turned her imploring big blue-green eyes to her sister. "Elizabeth, please, *please*, can't you do a twin switch with me? Just this one time?"

"Absolutely, categorically *no*," Elizabeth responded. Usually Jessica could talk her into just about anything, but today Elizabeth felt majorly fed up. She was in no mood for her twin's cajoling.

"Please, just this one time?" Jessica begged. "I promise, Liz, I'll *never* ask you to do anything like this again."

Elizabeth shook her head, wondering how many times she had heard that before. "Jessica, you got yourself into this situation," she said firmly. "You've got to get yourself out of it."

"Fine," Jessica huffed, turning up the radio and putting her foot on the accelerator. She drove in stony silence all the way to Calico Drive.

But as she pulled into the driveway, Jessica turned to her one last time. "So do you think you can do just this one little, *tiny* thing for me?" she asked hopefully.

"Jessica, the answer is no," Elizabeth said firmly. "Read my lips. N-O." She pulled open the door and breezed out of the Jeep.

Elizabeth heard Jessica slam the car door behind her. *Fine,* Elizabeth thought, *let her be angry. There's no way I'm going to fall for another of her crazy schemes!*

Chapter 7

How in the world did I get talked into this?
Elizabeth wondered for the hundredth time that
evening as she and Cameron walked into Chez
Paul, a ritzy French restaurant in downtown L.A.
She was wearing the same dress as her twin, and
she had done her hair and makeup just like
Jessica's.

Elizabeth heaved a sigh. It was bad enough that
she had to waste her evening parading around as
her twin, but she had to be *dressed* like Jessica as
well—which meant she was wearing a tiny black
halter dress barely bigger than a cloth napkin. Not
only that, her face also felt like it was going to
crack off under the weight of all her makeup. The
only thing she felt comfortable with was her hair-
style. Her golden-blond hair was swept up high on
her head, a few curled tendrils hanging loose.

"After you, mademoiselle," Cameron said gallantly, holding the door open for her. Elizabeth gave him a gracious smile, walking ahead of him into the elegant room. As they headed for the maître d's stand, Elizabeth yanked at the material of her dress, trying to cover her upper thighs. She felt as though everybody in the restaurant was staring at her.

Elizabeth shook her head. She couldn't believe Jessica had managed to talk her into this. Even though she had come into Elizabeth's room and whined about her dilemma for two hours straight, Elizabeth hadn't broken down. But then Jessica had laid a thick guilt trip on Elizabeth, explaining how she'd been sticking up for her sister during Todd and Simone's modeling sessions. "I told the Stick straight to her face that I thought she was despicable for going out with my sister's boyfriend," Jessica had said. "And I'm not even *talking* to Todd. How can you refuse to help me, your *twin*, when I've been doing nothing but standing up for you?" Guilt always got Elizabeth, and Jessica knew it. She sighed. Her sister was certainly the master of manipulation.

As Cameron conferred with the maître d', Elizabeth took in the plush surroundings. Fortunately for Jessica, Chez Paul was a large two-story restaurant, and Cameron and Quentin had reservations on different floors. Painted grape vines trailed across the mint green walls, and the tables were covered with elegant white tablecloths.

Each table was adorned with a crystal bud vase holding a single red rose. The elegantly-dressed clientele spoke in hushed voices, and only the clink of wine glasses could be heard above the low din of the crowd.

"This way, please," said a waiter in a black tuxedo.

Cameron took her arm and led her through the crowded dining room. "Better than Chez Bench, huh?" he whispered in her ear.

"Uh-huh," Elizabeth said, forcing a laugh. Unfortunately, she had no idea what he was talking about.

The waiter directed them to an intimate candlelit table in the corner, and Cameron held Elizabeth's chair for her. She slid into her seat, relieved to hide her bare thighs under the tablecloth.

Elizabeth scanned her menu, feeling a little intimidated by the refined selection. All of the entrees were in French, but fortunately there were English translations as well. Elizabeth's eyes widened as she took in the extravagant prices. She couldn't believe Jessica would have the gall to invite Cameron to come to such an expensive restaurant. After all, he worked in the mail room for a living. The guy couldn't exactly be made of money. But Cameron didn't seem fazed by the menu at all.

"I've heard the foie gras is very good here," Cameron said. Then he winked at her. "Too bad they don't serve hamburgers and fries."

Elizabeth relaxed, giving Cameron a genuine smile. "I know what you mean," she said. "I wouldn't mind having a burger and a shake from the Dairi Burger, a popular hangout in Sweet Valley."

"Tell you what, Jess," Cameron said. "Next time we go out, I'll let you treat me to a deluxe strawberry milkshake."

Elizabeth laughed. "You got it."

She ran an index finger down the elaborate entrees on the menu, trying to make up her mind. Then a devious thought occurred to her. Calamari was one of Elizabeth's favorite dishes and one which Jessica happened to despise. A small smile played on her lips. She would order it to punish Jessica for putting her in such an awkward situation. Elizabeth looked at the appetizers, searching for a few things Jessica hated as well. With a smile, she snapped her menu shut.

"So what are you going to have, Jessica?" Cameron asked.

"I thought I'd have the frog legs first." She smiled devilishly. "I love French delicacies."

Cameron nodded approvingly. "Ah, a woman with taste," he said. But despite his words, his eyes were dancing with laughter, as if he didn't take any of it seriously.

An elegant waiter appeared at their table. "*Bonsoir*," he said with a slight bow. "Have you made your selections?"

Cameron nodded, placing their orders in perfect French. Elizabeth looked at him oddly. For someone who worked in the mail room, this guy was pretty cultured. He seemed perfectly at ease in the elegant surroundings, as if he'd been frequenting posh French restaurants for years.

"Very good, sir," the waiter said, whisking the menus away.

Cameron winked. "Zee vaitor eez gone," he said in an exaggerated French accent. "Now vee can be ourselves."

Elizabeth laughed. Despite her initial reluctance, she was actually beginning to enjoy herself. Cameron was obviously a great guy. Jessica was crazy to risk him for Quentin the Jerk.

Cameron looked at her with a glint in his deep brown eyes. "I have to say, besides the fact that I know you're a beautiful girl who wants to be a model, I don't really know anything about you." He smiled, the tiny lines around his eyes crinkling.

Elizabeth swallowed hard, trying to think how Jessica would respond. She would smile coquettishly and say something funny and flirty. But what? Elizabeth stared at him blankly.

Fortunately Cameron kept talking. "So, what do you do when you're not looking and acting like a supermodel?"

Elizabeth exhaled slowly, realizing she had been holding her breath. "Well, I'm a pretty active member of Pi Beta Alpha, one of the sororities at

Sweet Valley High," she said. Elizabeth was a member as well, having been talked into joining the sorority by Jessica. But she never attended the meetings, and she had no idea what the girls' current activities were. "We . . . we're doing a fundraiser on Saturday," Elizabeth improvised quickly. "It's a car wash to raise money for charity."

Cameron grinned. "Maybe I'll come by Sweet Valley to have my car cleaned this weekend."

Elizabeth changed the subject, hoping he would forget about the car wash by the time dinner was over. "And I'm also the cocaptain of the cheerleading squad."

Cameron whistled underneath his breath. "You're the cocaptain of the squad?" he asked. He leaned in closer. "You know, I used to play soccer in high school, and the cheerleaders really helped to psych me up. I noticed that the moves are a lot more complicated than one might think."

"Yeah, they are," Elizabeth said brightly. "We even went to Nationals last season. We came in second."

"What are some of your most difficult moves?" Cameron asked, looking sincerely interested. He picked up the carafe of water and filled both his and Elizabeth's glasses.

Elizabeth gulped. When Jessica had quit the cheerleading squad because of Heather Mallone, her sworn enemy and cocaptain, she had formed her own squad to take to Nationals. She had talked

Elizabeth into joining her team, and Elizabeth had trained with the rest of the girls. Elizabeth racked her brains, trying to remember a move. She pictured leaps and splits, but she couldn't recollect any of the names. "Uh, pyramids are always hard," she replied lamely.

"What kind of pyramids?" Cameron asked.

Elizabeth's eyes widened. She couldn't believe that she was sitting across from the one guy in the history of the world who took an interest in cheerleading. "Um, well, two-two-two pyramids are pretty tough," she said, making up the move.

Cameron's brow furrowed. "Two-two-two? What does that mean?"

"Uh, two girls on each tier," Elizabeth explained, swallowing hard.

"That must be tough," Cameron said. "There's no balance on the bottom." He picked up his glass of water and took a drink.

Elizabeth nodded, glancing surreptitiously at her watch. She breathed a sigh of relief when she saw it was nine P.M.—time to meet Jessica in the bathroom so they could switch dates. "If you'll excuse me," she said, scraping her chair back and jumping up.

"Yeah, it was tough at the beginning," Quentin said, leaning back and crossing his long legs. He took a sip of his aperitif and shook his shaggy blond waves over his shoulder. "Calvin's the one who really gave me my first break. I did some test shots for him, and after that, well—" he gave her a smug smile, "I guess you could say the rest is history."

Calvin, Jessica thought in disgust. She stared out the window, phasing out as Quentin continued to go on and on about himself. She and Quentin were seated on the second floor at an elegant table overlooking Hollywood Boulevard. For the last half hour, he'd given her a complete bio of himself—all the great designers he'd worked with, all the beautiful models he'd photographed, and all the famous people he knew.

"Yes, I've worked with about every big name in the fashion industry," Quentin continued. "Chanel, St. Laurent, Givenchy." He ticked off the names on his fingers as he spoke. "And I've shot about every famous model there is."

Somebody should shoot you, Jessica thought.

"Tatiana, Marisa, Izzy," Quentin said, listing the supermodels he'd photographed.

Jessica shifted in her seat, growing more and more irritated by the moment. She was sick of hearing about Quentin's success, and she was sick of hearing about beautiful models who were too important to have last names.

"And of course, Simone," Quentin continued. "The first time we worked together was on a Chanel shoot."

Jessica sighed. She hadn't eaten anything since lunch, and sharp hunger pains were shooting through her stomach. The waiter was hovering politely in the corner, ready to take their order at the snap of a finger. But they hadn't even opened their menus yet.

The waiter caught her eye and hurried to the table, almost bowing as he greeted them. "May I take your order, Monsieur Berg?"

Quentin looked irritated and shook his head quickly, waving the waiter away.

Jessica rolled her eyes as the waiter hurried back to his spot in the corner. Obviously Monsieur Berg was used to making people wait for him.

"Now where was I?" he asked.

"You were talking about your Chanel shoot," Jessica said with a sigh.

"Ah yes, that was one of my most difficult shoots," Quentin said.

Jessica tuned him out and stared out the window at the elegant figures hurrying by on the street. She had known that Quentin was a bit of a jerk and a control freak, but she hadn't realized just how pretentious he was. When she and Elizabeth switched, Jessica decided, she'd tell her sister to spend the rest of the evening with Quentin. Otherwise, Jessica would die of boredom. Or starvation.

As the thought materialized, Jessica looked up at the antique brass clock on the wall. It was after nine o'clock. She was already five minutes late to meet Elizabeth in the bathroom.

"Uh, could you excuse me for a moment?" Jessica asked, pushing back her chair.

"Yes, of course," Quentin said, looking preoccupied.

What a relief, Jessica thought as she picked up her black pearl bag and headed for the stairs. She didn't know if she could stand one more moment of his insufferable company.

But then she heard Quentin's voice behind her. "Jessica, can you come back here for a moment?"

Jessica sighed, turning reluctantly back to the table.

"I was watching you walk away," Quentin said. "You've definitely got a model's carriage—good posture, long stride." He rubbed his chin thoughtfully. "You don't have the height for runway modeling, but I'm sure we could take some fantastic prints."

Jessica's spirits brightened. "Really?" she breathed.

"But we don't want to talk business over our meal," Quentin said. "Why don't we discuss your future as a model over dessert?"

Jessica flashed him a covergirl smile, deciding on the spot that she *did* want to return to this date after all. Quentin was the one who could help her. Cameron was just an amusing diversion.

"Man, I've never seen such a close game!" Kevin Anderson said on Friday night, referring to

103

the Southern California state championship high-school football game the night before.

"Me neither!" Shane Maddox agreed. "That was an *awesome* last pass. I thought the fans were going to bring down the stadium."

Enid sighed and took a bite of her cheese-burger. She and Maria were on their blind double date at Bobo's Burger Barn, a low-key restaurant in downtown Sweet Valley where you could draw on the paper tablecloths with crayons.

Kevin was certainly cute, with longish sandy blond hair and hazel eyes, but he was more inter-ested in Shane's guy talk than in anything Enid had to say. And even though Shane and Maria made a stunning couple, Shane didn't seem to realize that Maria was there at all. It turned out the two boys were both former football players who had just graduated from rival high schools, and they had spent the last hour in a heated discussion about sports.

"Yeah, the Panthers took a beating last season," Kevin was saying. "It's because they had a weak de-fense—they gave away too much yardage."

"I thought Derek Mallone was going to be able to pull them through," Shane responded. "But I guess a quarterback can't carry the whole team."

Enid turned in the boys' direction, trying to look interested. "Aren't the Panthers the team from Palisades?" she asked. The guys didn't even notice she had spoken.

Maria cleared her throat. "Enid asked you a question. She wanted to know if that's the team from Allboysarejerks High."

"Huh?" Shane asked, looking at Maria as if he just realized she was sitting next to him. "Yeah, that's right."

Enid and Maria snickered, but the boys were already engrossed in their conversation again.

Enid yawned and stuffed the last of her fries into her mouth. Then she took a long draw on her soda and pushed her plate away. Maria picked out a crayon from the jar and drew a fuschia-colored curly-haired Enid on the tablecloth. In the cartoon Enid's right hand was held up to her open mouth.

Enid picked out a blue crayon, and then leaned over and added a dialogue balloon to the cartoon figure. She wrote "yawn" inside the bubble. Enid heard Maria giggle and refused to look at her for fear of laughing.

Forcing herself to keep a straight face, Enid turned back to the boys' conversation. Shane was designing a football move on the table with a green crayon, detailing a particularly difficult maneuver.

Then she felt Maria nudge her. She glanced over and looked at the tablecloth. Maria had drawn two stupid-looking football players holding clubs like cavemen, with a dialogue bubble over one caveman's head. "Like, cool, man," the bubble said.

Enid burst out laughing and jumped up. "Excuse me, I've got to use the powder room," she said over the din of Kevin and Shane's conversation. Maria quickly followed. The boys nodded without looking at them.

In the bathroom, the girls doubled over with laughter. "Hey, don't you guys go to Allguysarestupid High?" Enid asked, imitating Shane's voice.

"Duh, huh?" Maria answered.

Enid shook her head. "I thought you said Kevin was quiet. He hasn't stopped talking since we got here." She pulled a tube of mauve lipstick out of her black minibackpack and pursed her lips in the mirror.

"I didn't say he was quiet," Maria said, retying the blue bandanna in her hair. "I said we had nothing in common."

"That's an understatement," Enid agreed, smacking her lips on a tissue. "The only thing he and I have in common is that we both know you."

Maria sighed and leaned back against a sink. "It's too bad they both turned out to be such total duds," she said, shaking her head. "They *are* pretty cute."

"I can't understand how seemingly intelligent guys can care more about hockey fights and football tackles than they do about holding interesting conversation with two totally hot babes," Enid said.

"Well, it's their loss," Maria declared.

Enid made a face of distaste. "I can't stand the thought of going back in there. If I hear the word *football* one more time, I think I might explode."

"Who said anything about going back in there?" Maria asked, a devilish smile on her face.

Enid smiled back. "Are you thinking what I think you're thinking?"

"Definitely," Maria affirmed. "Girl, we are outta here."

Enid giggled as she and Maria hurried out of the bathroom and snuck out the back entrance. "I wonder when the boys will notice we're gone," she said.

Maria shrugged. "Probably tomorrow morning."

Chapter 8

Elizabeth paced the length of the spacious powder room, wondering where her sister was. The women's room was just as elegant as the fancy restaurant. Pink marble sinks lined the wall, with a long beige leather couch opposite them. A full-length antique mirror stood in the corner, and Elizabeth cringed every time she caught sight of her dolled-up reflection in it.

Elizabeth heard the door open and wheeled around. It was Jessica, her face pink with excitement. "Jessica Wakefield, you're ten minutes late!" she exclaimed. "What in the world am I supposed to say I was doing in here?"

Jessica winced. "Liz, I'm sorry. Quentin started talking about my modeling career, and I couldn't get away," she explained. "Just say you were freshening up. Remember, you *are* me after all."

Elizabeth sighed, glancing at her skimpy dress in the standing mirror. "How can I forget?"

Jessica set her handbag on the counter and pulled out a cosmetic bag. Then she opened it and turned it upside down, dumping an array of jars and tubes on the counter. Closing one eye, she carefully applied plum eye shadow to an eyelid. "I almost perished of boredom out there. Quentin hasn't stopped talking about himself for a minute. We haven't even had time to order."

Elizabeth smiled to herself, anticipating Jessica's reaction when she saw her dish of frogs legs and calamari. "Don't worry, I'll order for you," she said.

"Thanks, Liz," Jessica said, outlining her lips with a pink lip pencil.

Elizabeth sunk down in the couch. "What in the world is Chez Bench, by the way?" she asked.

Jessica's brow furrowed. "Huh?" she asked, forming an O with her lips and painting them with crimson lipstick.

"A restaurant you went to with Cameron?" Elizabeth prompted.

"Oh," Jessica said, throwing her lipstick back into her cosmetic bag. "That's just a joke. Cameron and I ate on the bench outside the *Mode* building one day, and he called it Chez Bench."

Elizabeth laughed. "That's actually pretty funny," she said. "Jessica, Cameron's a terrific guy. I think you should just bag Quentin and stay with him."

"I wish I could," Jessica said, pulling out a few wispy strands to frame her face. "But Quentin said he wants to discuss my future after dinner."

Elizabeth tapped a foot on the ground, looking at her watch nervously. "Jess, don't you think we should get back to our dates? The guys might send an emergency squad in here."

Jessica waved a dismissive hand. "Oh, Lizzie, you don't know the first thing about dating etiquette. Guys are *supposed* to be kept waiting. In fact, that's what they do best. They wait."

Elizabeth shook her head. "Well, I don't," she said firmly, hopping up. "I'm going upstairs."

Jessica grabbed her arm. "OK, but just prep me on your conversation with Cameron first. Is there anything I should know about it?"

Elizabeth fell back down on the couch. "Not really," she said. "We mostly talked about French philosophers—you know, Sartre, Camus, and Descartes."

Jessica's mouth dropped open. "You didn't!"

Elizabeth rolled her eyes. "Of course not, you goof," she said. "Don't worry. We just talked about normal stuff—Pi Beta Alpha and cheerleading."

Jessica looked worried. "What about them?" she asked cautiously.

"Well, I told Cameron that Pi Beta Alpha was having a car wash for charity this weekend."

"A charity drive?" Jessica asked. "But there's no way the sorority would do that."

Elizabeth shrugged. "Well, he doesn't know that." Then she looked down at the ground. "The only thing is—he might drive to Sweet Valley to get his car washed on Saturday."

"Oh, boy," Jessica sighed. "Anything else I should know about?"

Elizabeth shook her head. "Otherwise, we just talked about cheerleading moves. I told him the most difficult maneuver was a two-by-two-by-two pyramid."

"A *what?*" Jessica asked, aghast.

Elizabeth glared at her sister, getting annoyed. "Look, Jessica, you're lucky I'm here at all. If you aren't happy with my conversational skills, maybe you should go on your own dates next time."

"OK, OK," Jessica grumbled. "But a two-by-two-by-two pyramid?" She shook her head. "It isn't possible."

"Don't worry," Elizabeth reassured her. "He's a guy. He doesn't know anything about cheerleading."

Jessica sighed. "Fine. But watch what you say to Quentin, OK?"

"So what's it like having a twin sister?" Cameron asked as soon as Jessica sat down.

Jessica was thrown off kilter, but recovered quickly. "Oh, it's OK," she said, avoiding his eyes and taking a bite out of her appetizer. She grimaced and almost spat it out. Her eyes widened as she recognized the rubbery dish—frogs legs—

111

gross! Jessica's eyes narrowed suspiciously. Elizabeth obviously ordered this on purpose.

Cameron looked concerned. "What's wrong? I thought frogs legs were one of your favorite dishes." He looked at her carefully. "Didn't you say you loved French delicacies?"

Jessica swallowed hard. "Uh, yeah, yeah, definitely," she said. "Just went down the wrong pipe." She forced a smile on her face and took another bite, trying hard not to gag at the foreign taste.

"Must be weird to have a twin," Cameron went on. "Like when you go into the bathroom and look in the mirror, it's almost like you're looking at someone else."

Jessica almost choked on her food this time. She grabbed a glass of water.

"Do you ever have an identity crisis?" Cameron asked, cutting into his fried mushrooms.

Jessica looked straight into his eyes, wondering if he knew what was going on. But he just stared back at her, his deep brown eyes not giving anything anyway. Then she dismissed the possibility. He couldn't possibly know. Her plan was going smoothly.

Cameron waved a hand in front of her face. "Jess? Did somebody steal your mind while you were in the bathroom?"

Jessica laughed. "Oh, sorry," she said. "I'm just a bit distracted tonight."

"I was asking you if you ever have an identity

crisis," Cameron repeated, taking a bite of his appetizer. Jessica looked at it enviously, but Cameron didn't offer her any. "Umm, delicious," he said, mopping up the plate with a piece of French bread.

"Actually, no," Jessica said, forcing her mind off the food. "Even though Elizabeth and I look identical, we're entirely different. Elizabeth's more serious—and studious—than I am. I like to be in the center of the action, and she's more of a behind-the-scenes kind of person."

"So that's why she's in editorial and you're in the art department—where the cameras are?"

Jessica nodded. "Elizabeth wants to be a writer someday."

"And you want to be a model," Cameron said.

Jessica shrugged. "Or an actress."

Just then their food arrived, and Jessica heaved a sigh of relief to have the conversation cut off.

"*Pour le monsieur, un steak frites,*" said the waiter, setting down a red steak and french fries before Cameron. Jessica's mouth watered at the tantalizing dish.

"*Et pour vous, Mademoiselle, le calamari,*" the waiter said with a flourish, lifting the lid off a steaming dish and setting it before her.

Jessica stared at the platter in alarm, trying to figure out what it was. It was viscous and white with a faintly purple tinge, and the whole thing was covered in some kind of lemon butter sauce. Then she realized what it was. *Squid!* Elizabeth had struck again.

113

"Bon appetit!" Cameron said, lifting a glass in the air. He picked up his knife and fork and cut off a piece of steak, biting into it heartily.

"Bon appetit!" Jessica echoed despondently. She slowly broke up her food in little pieces, wondering how she could get out of eating it.

"How is it?" Cameron asked.

Jessica took a tiny bit and forced herself to chew it. It was worse than she had expected. It had a salty sea taste and a horrible slimy texture. Jessica swallowed hard and took a gulp of water. "Um, delicious, thank you," she coughed.

"Mine too," Cameron said, spooning some Dijon mustard on his plate. He stabbed a pile of fries with his fork, dipping them into the mustard. Jessica stared hungrily, wishing he would offer her a bite. While Cameron devoured his steak, Jessica pushed the pieces of shredded squid around her plate, trying to make it look like she had eaten some of it.

Jessica heaved a sigh of relief when the waiter took their dishes away. Fortunately, she'd managed to eat only a few bites of the revolting dish.

Cameron smiled at her, taking her hand in his. "Jessica, I'm so glad you came out with me tonight. It's good to see you in the real world."

His hand was warm over hers. His brown eyes gazed deep into her eyes, and she felt her stomach flutter. As Cameron leaned forward to kiss her, she glanced down at the watch on his wrist. Ten o'clock. Time for a twin switch.

Jessica kissed Cameron quickly, then pulled away. "Better save something for dessert," she said lightly, pushing back her chair.

She sighed as she walked away from the table, feeling like Cinderella at the ball. Things were just beginning to heat up between her and Cameron, and now Elizabeth got to have him.

Elizabeth sat down and flashed Cameron a sincere smile, grateful to be back at his table. Quentin was one of the most tedious, unbearable, egotistical bores she had ever encountered. Elizabeth especially hated the way he kept raving about Simone, her least favorite person in the world—aside from Todd. Not only did Quentin keep talking about what a prima model Simone was, but about her exceptional beauty as well. Elizabeth had just felt sick during the entire conversation.

Just then the waiter arrived with a luscious-looking dessert tray in his hand. He set down two plates of chocolate mousse on the table and two cups of espresso.

"I took the liberty of ordering dessert," Cameron explained. "Is that OK?"

"Of course," Elizabeth said, her mouth watering. "It looks fantastic."

The waiter bowed slightly and turned away.

"*Mmm,*" Elizabeth murmured, taking a bite of the rich chocolate cake. "This is delicious." *Actually,* she thought, *except for the excruciating hour at Quentin's table, I've kind of had a good time this evening.* Her frog legs were exquisite, and she'd really enjoyed Cameron's company.

"Thanks for dinner," Elizabeth said sincerely as she and Cameron walked out of the restaurant.

"It was my pleasure," Cameron responded, taking her hand in his and kissing the back of it. Then he fingered the silver watch dangling on her wrist. "Hey, nice watch."

"Oh, I've had it forever," Elizabeth said. "I got it as a birthday gift from my grandparents years ago."

Cameron nodded, as if Elizabeth's statement confirmed something that he had been thinking. Then he took both her hands in his and leaned toward her.

For a moment, Elizabeth panicked. Was he going to kiss her? What should she do? She couldn't exactly push him away and run off. But he just smiled at her and kissed her lightly on the cheek. "Thanks for a lovely evening, *Elizabeth*," he said.

Then he winked and disappeared into the night.

Elizabeth's mouth dropped open. How did he know she wasn't Jessica? Then it hit her. Her watch! She had forgotten that Jessica never wore a watch. Elizabeth sighed as she walked toward the Jeep in the parking lot. Jessica was going to kill her.

Chapter 9

"This is it," Jessica said, pointing to the Wakefield's split-level house on Calico Drive.

Quentin expertly pulled his silver Mercedes to a stop in front of the curb.

"Thanks for a lovely evening," Jessica said, flashing Quentin a fake smile.

"The pleasure was all mine," Quentin responded suavely.

Jessica put her hand on the door handle, anxious to get away from Quentin and his overblown ego. Not only had he talked about himself nonstop all through dinner, but all during the car ride home as well.

But Quentin reached over and took her hand in his. His other hand trailed slowly down her neck, sending a slow shiver of disgust down Jessica's spine.

"I like you, Jessica," Quentin declared. "You've got style and guts. I really think you're going to go places."

Now Quentin had her full attention. "You do?" Jessica asked, her blue-green eyes sparkling.

"I do," he whispered, kissing her softly on the cheek. He followed with a trail of soft kisses along her neck and ear. Then he leaned forward and captured her lips in his.

Jessica closed her eyes and returned his kiss, trying to lose herself in the moment. But all she could think of was Cameron. She pictured his laughing brown eyes and the dimple in his chin. She thought of the last time he had kissed her— unexpectedly—in the mail room, and of the sparks of lightning that had coursed through her entire body. She moaned and wrapped her arms around Quentin, kissing him harder.

"Mmm, Jessica," Quentin murmured, increasing the pressure on her lips.

Jessica spoke to Cameron in her mind. *Cameron, it's almost like I'm kissing you. Are you thinking the same thing while you're kissing—*

Jessica shivered suddenly and pulled out of Quentin's grasp, hit by a horrible thought.

"Jessica, are you OK?" Quentin asked.

Jessica nodded, feeling the blood rush out of her face. "Yeah, sorry, I just got a sudden chill. It must be the night air."

"Well, let me take care of that," Quentin said,

turning on the engine and rolling up the window. He wrapped both his arms around her and rubbed her back slowly.

As Quentin held her in his arms, Jessica fixated on Elizabeth and Cameron. She only hoped that Elizabeth wasn't receiving a passionate kiss from Cameron at the moment. But if Cameron believed Elizabeth were Jessica . . . Jessica pushed the thought away. The thought of Cameron kissing her sister made her skin crawl.

Finally Jessica pulled out of Quentin's arms. "I better go in," she said, leaning over and giving him a peck on the cheek.

"Sleep well," Quentin said. Then he winked. "After all, you want to look your best tomorrow."

Jessica turned the handle and pushed the door open. But then she stopped and faced Quentin again. "Do you really think I have a chance to end up in the magazine?" she asked.

Quentin nodded. "Don't worry," he assured her. "I'll make sure of it."

"See you tomorrow," Jessica said, hopping out of the car.

It's all worth it, she assured herself as she hurried up the front walk. Quentin was the key to her career. He was going to make her a supermodel.

Late Friday night, Todd lay in bed fully dressed, listening to the sounds of the sleeping house. He could hear the dishwasher humming in

119

the kitchen and the whirring of the heat vents. But otherwise, the house was silent. His parents had gone to bed an hour ago.

Todd glanced at his alarm clock—eleven P.M. It was time to go. He slid soundlessly to the ground and slipped his feet into his waiting shoes. He carefully picked up his brown leather jacket from the chair and stuffed his wallet into his pants pockets. Holding his breath, Todd stood perfectly still, listening. But nothing stirred in the house.

Todd padded soundlessly down the hall and listened at the door of his parents' room. He could hear his mother's even breathing and his dad's snoring. Then he inched his way down the hall and tiptoed down the winding staircase. A wooden step creaked, and Todd stopped. He strained his ears, breathing a sigh of relief when he could make out the faint sound of his father's snoring. Todd continued down, remaining close to the wall to prevent the steps from squeaking.

He carefully pulled open the front door and crept outside, slowly shutting it behind him.

The night was clear and cool, and Todd pulled his jacket on, taking deep breaths of the balmy air. A feeling of freedom surged through him as he headed for his BMW across the street. Todd pulled the door open and slid in, closing it quietly behind him.

As he turned on the accelerator, Todd felt heady with excitement. It was eleven P.M. and he was on his way *out,* heading to downtown L.A. for a date with a gorgeous supermodel. He couldn't wait to tell Aaron and Winston all about it. They would turn green with envy.

Glancing in the rearview window, Todd turned up the collar of his jacket and fluffed out his hair. He looked cool and dark, he thought in satisfaction. He would fit in perfectly with the late-night Los Angeles crowd. Todd flicked on the radio and turned the knob, stopping at a techno station. The pulsing beat filled his body, and a jolt of adrenaline coursed through him.

This night is much more exciting than making out with Elizabeth at Miller's Point, Todd thought to himself. If he'd gone out with *her* tonight, he'd already be in bed by now.

Elizabeth was too uptight anyway. After all, Simone wouldn't make such a big deal about it if he kissed someone else.

Elizabeth is just a girl, Todd decided. *Simone is a woman.*

Jessica burst into the house with one thought on her mind—Elizabeth and Cameron. She hadn't even thought about the goodnight kiss before. If she had, she would have rethought the whole evening. She might share dates with her sister, but she didn't share kisses.

Jessica bounded up the stairs two steps at a time and burst into Elizabeth's room. Nobody was there. She flicked on the overhead light, blinking as she adjusted to the glare. The bed was still perfectly made like Elizabeth left it every morning.

Jessica began to panic. What if Elizabeth and Cameron had gone out afterward somewhere? What if they had gone to Miller's Point? What if Elizabeth really liked him?

Jessica, calm yourself, she told herself sternly. *Elizabeth would never do that to you. She would never steal a boyfriend from you.* But then Jessica thought of Elizabeth's secret affair with Ken Matthews. When Jessica and Ken were going out, Elizabeth had pulled a twin switch and had gone on a date with Ken to see if she still had feelings for him. And she had kissed him.

Jessica's feeling of foreboding burst into full blossom and she flew down the steps. "Liz, where are you?" she called.

She ran into the kitchen and turned on the light. The cheery copper-colored room was empty and spotless. "What is this, a ghost house?" she muttered.

Jessica hurried into the living room, her panic mounting. Then she heaved a sigh of relief. Elizabeth was curled up under an Afghan blanket on the sofa. "There you are!" she said in relief, sinking into the armchair in the corner.

"Huh?" Elizabeth asked in a groggy voice, opening her eyes to slits.

Jessica couldn't stand one more moment of waiting. She drummed her fingers on the arm of the chair. "So, did he kiss you goodnight?" she asked.

"What?" Elizabeth asked, wrapping the blanket around her shoulders and pulling herself up to a sitting position. She ran her fingers through her disheveled hair.

"Cameron," Jessica explained impatiently. "Did he kiss you?"

Elizabeth rolled her eyes. "You're welcome, Jessica," she said. "It was a pleasure for me to cover for you." Then she smiled devilishly. "Did you enjoy your meal?"

Jessica scowled. "Very funny, Liz. Yes, it was delicious. Now, you could please just answer the question?"

A strange glint came into Elizabeth's eyes. "Of course he kissed me," she said. "Do you really think Cameron would go out on a date with you without kissing you goodnight?"

A horrified chill crept slowly down Jessica's spine. "Did you kiss him back?"

Elizabeth shrugged, yawning. "Well, I didn't want to, but I had to. You know. So he would think I was you."

Jessica was furious. And hurt. Elizabeth had actually betrayed her. "I can't believe you kissed my date! What a disgusting thing to do!"

"Well, you don't want him to think you're a bad kisser, do you?" Elizabeth asked, her face all innocence.

Jessica stared at her opened mouth. She couldn't believe Elizabeth would do this to her. Her own sister. Her *twin*.

"Jess, he's a great kisser," Elizabeth said in a dreamy voice. "He's tender, but passionate at the same time." She sighed and snuggled into the Afghan. "I can see why you like him so much."

Jessica stood up, staring at her sister in horror. Had Elizabeth become an alien being? Had she transformed into psycho twin? Jessica threw up her arms. "Look, I don't want to hear another word." With that, she stomped up the steps.

She heard the sounds of Elizabeth's footsteps behind her and hurried more quickly down the hall.

"Wait, Jess —" Elizabeth said from behind her.

"Leave me alone," Jessica said, slipping into her bedroom and slamming shut the door behind her.

But Elizabeth just opened the door and followed her anyway, a slight grin on her face. "Do you know how many *l*'s there are in the word *gullible*?" she asked.

"Elizabeth, don't talk to me," Jessica said, storming into the bathroom and slamming the door behind her. Her whole body was heated up, and she was trembling slightly. Jessica wrapped her arms around her body. She couldn't believe that Cameron would kiss her sister. And that Elizabeth would betray her like that. She leaned her head against the door, feeling totally defeated. Then Elizabeth's words penetrated her consciousness.

Jessica quickly pushed open the door. Elizabeth was sitting against the wall on Jessica's bed, casually thumbing through a fashion magazine.

"What did you say?" Jessica asked.

"I asked you how many *l*'s there were in *gullible*," Elizabeth said with a smile.

Jessica heaved a sigh of relief and flopped down on the floor, pushing a pile of clothing out of her way. "So you didn't kiss him," she said.

"Of course not, silly," Elizabeth affirmed.

Jessica collapsed dramatically onto the floor. "What a relief!" she said. Then she sat up again, her good spirits quickly restored. "Well, it all worked out perfectly," she said. "Now I'm going to get my shoot with Quentin and go out with Cameron as well—"

"Not quite," Elizabeth said, cutting her off.

This time Elizabeth's face looked serious.

"Oh, no, what happened?" Jessica asked.

"The jig is up, Jess," Elizabeth said. "Cameron figured out that we pulled a twin switch." Elizabeth grimaced. "He noticed my watch."

"Drat," Jessica muttered. And it had all been going so well. *But then,* she thought diplomatically, *it could have been worse.* The most important thing was that Cameron didn't kiss Elizabeth goodnight.

Jessica shrugged. "Oh, well," she said. "I guess I'll just call him tomorrow and apologize. I'm sure he'll understand."

Elizabeth shook her head. "Jessica Wakefield, some times you are just too much."

Jessica gave her a dazzling grin. "I am, aren't I?"

Chapter 10

Elizabeth sat at a stool at the kitchen counter on Saturday afternoon, furiously chopping up vegetables for dinner. All day, the only thing she had been able to think about was Todd and Simone. She had woken up thinking about them, they had plagued her mind all morning, and now here they were again, tormenting her. She was beginning to see red. *Think of something else,* she commanded herself. *Think of Jessica and Cameron.* But as she viciously whacked a yellow squash, she couldn't help envisioning Simone's head.

The phone rang, and Elizabeth rushed to get it, grateful for a distraction from her disturbing thoughts. She wiping her hands on a dishrag and then picked up the receiver from the phone on the wall. "Hello?" she asked.

"Hello, Elizabeth, is that you?" a deep female

voice asked. Elizabeth recognized Leona at once.

"Hi, Leona!" Elizabeth said, surprised to hear from her on the weekend. She cradled the receiver in the crook of her neck and walked back to the kitchen counter, setting out a red and a yellow pepper on the cutting board. "So, are congratulations in order?"

"Not yet, but I'm working on it," Leona responded. "In fact, I had an inspiration last night. I'm going to lure Sam to a romantic weekend skiing in Lake Tahoe. I'm sure that once he's away from the city, he'll propose."

Elizabeth sliced through the red pepper. "Why don't you just ask him?" she suggested. "After all, he obviously appreciates liberated, independent women. I'm sure he'd be flattered."

Leona laughed, and her hearty voice came through the line. "Elizabeth, he would be terrified. And he would run for the hills. Believe me, men may put on a macho act, but inside they're like little boys. If a woman is *too* strong and independent, they get scared away. You see, essentially I'm asking him. But I'm letting him *think* he asked me."

"I see," Elizabeth said, not sure if she was convinced by Leona's logic. She scraped the slices of red and yellow peppers into a wooden salad bowl.

"I'm going to take Monday off as well," Leona asked. "If anybody asks, just tell them I'm sick."

"Uh, OK," Elizabeth said slowly.

"Thanks Elizabeth. You're a doll," Leona said. Then the phone clicked off.

Elizabeth hung up the phone slowly, feeling weird about the prospect of lying for her boss. Leona might be strong and independent, but she didn't seem to have much of a work ethic. Or a personal ethic either.

And that's why she's successful, Elizabeth thought in a moment of sudden clarity. *That's why she's on her way to the top.* People like Elizabeth—*nice* people—wouldn't get anywhere. They just would be betrayed and walked on.

Elizabeth sunk down in a chair at the kitchen table, feeling as though she had been cheated. She had always thought her ideals and integrity would get her somewhere. But, obviously, they were only in her way.

You're so naive, Elizabeth berated herself. *So, so naive.*

"My entire body hurts," Lila complained, sitting up in the chaise longue and stretching out her neck. It was Saturday afternoon, and Jessica and Lila were laying out by the pool in the Wakefield's backyard. Jessica was wearing a sleek new white one-piece bathing suit and Lila was outfitted in a floral bikini with a matching sarong.

Jessica raised an eyebrow. From the way Lila had been going on about her internship at Fowler Enterprises, you'd think she was doing manual labor, not working the switchboards.

"Must take a lot of effort to answer the

128

phones," Jessica said wryly, sitting up as well and reaching for a glass of iced tea on the side table between them.

"You have no idea," Lila said in a snooty tone. "I have to sit at the receptionist desk for eight hours a day, working the switchboard, directing clients, and answering phones. By the time five o'clock rolls around, I feel like I've been through a battle."

"You should try doing some *real* work," Jessica said. "Like moving fake boulders and lugging buckets of water around." Jessica picked up a bottle of sunblock, squeezed a bit on her palm, and began smoothing it on her face.

"At least you've got a *real* internship on a *real* fashion magazine," Lila responded. "I'm nothing more than a glorified secretary—for my *father*." Lila scowled as she picked up the bottle of sunblock. "No, I take that back. I'm not even glorified." She squeezed some of the lotion onto her palm, but then she dropped the bottle as if it were on fire. "Sunblock number 45? Jessica, are you crazy? What's the point of laying out if you block out *all* the rays?"

"The sun is good for your overall health," Jessica said pointedly. "But I have to protect my skin if I'm going to be a fashion model." She rubbed the rest of the lotion on her arms and shoulders.

Lila shook her head. "You got any baby oil around here?"

Jessica laughed and threw her a bottle of suntan oil.

129

"That's better," Lila said, sitting up and smoothing the oil on her golden-brown legs.

Jessica felt around the ground under her chair, searching for her tube of lip balm. "Well, if you hate it so much, why don't you ask your father for more responsibility?" she suggested, pursing her lips and running the lip balm along them. Jessica smacked her lips together, blanching at the coconut taste.

Lila looked at her aghast. "You mean, *work?*"

Jessica shook her head. "No, you're right. You might break a nail."

Lila sighed. "Actually, my father wants this to be a learning experience for me—he wants me to learn what it's like for the rest of the world."

"And have you learned anything?" Jessica asked.

"Definitely," Lila asserted, pushing her sunglasses on and leaning back in the chaise longue. "I am definitely meant to be rich and idle." She picked up her glass of iced tea and took a sip.

"I, on the other hand, am meant to be rich and working," Jessica said.

"Hmm?" Lila asked. Her eyes were closed and her face was lifted to the sun.

"Quentin promised to get me into the magazine," Jessica said.

Lila snorted. "I'll believe that when I see it."

"Don't worry, Lila. I'll still be your friend when I'm rich and famous," Jessica offered generously, lowering the chaise longue and laying her head back. Jessica closed her eyes, enjoying the luxurious feel of the hot sun beating down on her body.

"Thanks, Jess," Lila said flatly. "So does that mean you blew off Cameron?"

"Well, not exactly," Jessica said. She swung her feet off the chaise longue and sat up. Then she told Lila about the Cameron debacle of the night before. Jessica sighed when she was finished. "So, I guess I'll have to weasel my way out of it on Monday."

Lila turned her face to Jessica, covering her eyes from the sun. "Jess, if you really like this guy, I wouldn't wait until Monday."

"You're right," Jessica decided, jumping up. "I'll call him right now."

Jessica pushed open the sliding glass door and ran into the kitchen. A few minutes later, she reappeared, carrying a cellular phone and a telephone directory.

Jessica plopped down on the chair with the big white telephone book on her lap, leafing through the pages until she got to the S's. "Lila, there are like a thousand Smiths in here," she said in dismay.

"His last name is Smith?" Lila asked. "That's so stupid."

Jessica shook her head. Sometimes Lila's twisted logic defied a response. She ran a finger slowly down the dense column, peering at the small print. "Cagey, Caitlin, Caliban, Callum, Cary—Lila, there's no Cameron."

131

"I'll take care of this," Lila said. She picked up the cellular phone and pressed 4-1-1. "Yes, I'd like the number of a Mr. Cameron Smith, please." She admired her long shell pink manicured nails as she waited. "No, are you sure? OK, thank you."

Lila hung up the phone. "He's not listed. How strange," she said. "He must be too poor to have a phone."

Jessica frowned. "I guess that means I'll have to talk my way out of this mess at *Flair* on Monday." Then she shrugged. "Oh well. I'm sure it'll work out."

But somehow she had a feeling that Lila might be right. Monday might be too late. Jessica sighed. Maybe she really had blown her chances with Cameron after all.

Todd woke up late on Sunday morning. Feeling groggy, he sat up in bed rubbing his eyes. The sun was streaming through his window, and he could hear his parents downstairs talking over brunch. Sunday brunch was a tradition at the Wilkins's home. Todd stood up and picked up a crumpled pair of black jeans and a wrinkled wine-colored T-shirt from the floor, pulling them on quickly.

But then he ripped them off again. He went out to a club again Saturday night, and the cloying smell of cigarette smoke was in his hair and on his clothes. He threw on a navy blue bathrobe and hurried to the bathroom down the hall.

Ten minutes later, Todd headed down the steps, whistling to himself. He was wearing a clean pair of sweatpants and a T-shirt, and he was freshly shaven. He was beginning to enjoy this routine of going to bed late and getting up late. He couldn't believe how easy it was to sneak out. The night before he and Simone had gone to a trendy jazz club downtown, and he had actually enjoyed himself for the first time. He was getting to know some of the people in the model crowd she hung out with, and they seemed to like him.

"Good morning," Todd said cheerily as he walked into the kitchen.

"Morning, dear," his mother said with a smile. She was dressed casually, in jeans and a blazer, and her auburn hair was tied up in a green scarf.

"Mmm, looks great," Todd said, gazing appreciatively at the Sunday-morning spread. A large platter of scrambled eggs stood in the middle of the table, with a basket of homemade blueberry muffins next to it. His mother had fixed a fresh fruit salad as well, with cantaloupe, honeydew melon, and kiwi.

Todd sat down at his table and filled his plate.

"You're up late," his father remarked, looking up from the newspaper on his lap.

"Yeah, I was studying for a history test last night," Todd said, thinking quickly. He shrugged. "Since I couldn't go out, I figured I'd make the best of my time."

Todd could feel his face flushing and stared at his plate. He wasn't used to lying to his parents like this. But then, what was he supposed to do? If they were going to insist on imposing absolutely ridiculous rules, then he was going to have to find a way to get around them.

"Good thinking," his father said. The Italian coffeemaker began to hiss, and Todd's father stood up and went to the stove. He returned a moment later with two cups of espresso, setting one down in front of Mrs. Wilkins.

"I'm sorry we were so tough on you, Todd," his father said when he sat down. "But it's important for you to learn responsibility at a young age."

Todd nodded. "Don't worry, there are no hard feelings," he said. "I understand." But his father's kind words just added to his guilt, and now Todd really felt like a heel. His stabbed at the eggs on his plate with a fork, concentrating on his food. He felt his dad's piercing eyes on him, but he kept on eating steadily, trying to seem unconcerned.

"Would you like some more eggs, dear?" Mrs. Wilkins asked.

"Sure, thanks, Mom," Todd said, reaching out a hand for the platter.

"What's that?" Mr. Wilkins asked suddenly.

"What's what?" Todd asked, his heart began to sound a drumroll in his chest.

"That, the red stamp on your hand," Mr. Wilkins said, pointing at the back of Todd's right hand.

Todd looked down at his hand and gulped. The stamp from the club last night hadn't washed off in the shower. "Oh, that's nothing," he said quickly. "Just, just something from school on Friday."

Mr. Wilkins voice was cold. "You didn't have school on Friday."

Todd swallowed hard. "I meant last week—"

But Mr. Wilkins cut him off. "Don't bother, Todd. You didn't have a stamp on your hand yesterday." Mr. Wilkins frowned, disappointment marring his features. "It's from a club. You obviously snuck out last night."

Todd didn't respond. For a moment, there was total silence in the room. Todd sat perfectly still, waiting for his punishment. What were they going to do, ground him for the rest of his life?

When Todd's father spoke again, his voice was quiet and resolved. "Todd, I want you to listen to me. If you cross the line one more time, you're going to be in big trouble." He looked Todd straight in the eye. "Is that understood?"

"Yes, perfectly," Todd muttered, his face heating up in anger. He stared at the table, biting back a response. He felt guilty for lying to his parents, but he was also fed up with the way they were treating him. They were acting like he was an infant.

He felt as though the whole world had been dictating his actions lately. Elizabeth went nuts just because he had kissed Simone, and his parents were trying to completely control him. It wasn't as if he was doing anything wrong. He was just going out dancing at night. Simone was right. If he didn't assert himself, they'd always treat him like a child.

Todd stood up and threw down his napkin. "I think I've lost my appetite," he said. "Do you mind if I leave without finishing my breakfast . . . or won't I get any dessert?"

"Todd!" his mother exclaimed, looking shocked.

"Watch it," his father warned. "You're pushing it."

Todd shrugged, stalking out of the room. He grabbed his basketball and headed for the front door. He needed to work off some steam.

Chapter 11

"Where in the world is Simone?" Quentin demanded, throwing his hands in the air. He had been repeating the words like a mantra for the past two hours. He kicked at a rock in frustration, sending a cloud of dust in the air.

On the set, Jessica winced, holding back a cough. It was late Monday morning, and Quentin was totally stressed out because Simone was hours late and no one could get in touch with her. The morning's shoot was a Roman ruins scene, and the set was fully constructed. Big gray rocks stood in front of a crumbling acropolis, and five black cats were running around the ruins. The lights were ready as well, and everybody on the art crew was standing around, waiting for Simone.

Quentin stalked back to his camera and peered through the lens. "Isn't somebody going to adjust those lights?" he roared, pointing to a blue lighting fixture strung up in the corner.

"Yes, sir, Mr. Berg," responded an assistant quickly, hurrying over to the light.

"Uh-oh, looks like Quentin's on the warpath," Shelly whispered to Jessica.

"I think we better stay out of his way," Jessica whispered back.

Quentin looked at his watch for the hundredth time. "This is an extremely important shoot," he ranted to everybody and nobody, "and we've only got this morning to shoot it."

"*Mrrrw!*" screeched a skinny cat, jumping from the wall of the acropolis onto Quentin's shoulder.

"Would somebody *please* take care of these animals?" Quentin shouted, flinging the cat off his shoulder. The cat yowled and went flying to the ground.

"Here, kitty," Jessica called, quickly gathering the animal up in her arms. "C'mere, kitties," she said, clucking her tongue as she poured dry cat food into a plastic blue bowl. The four other cats quickly ran to her, rubbing against her leg. "OK, there's enough for all of you," she said soothingly.

Shelly joined her quickly, filling a couple of bowls with milk.

"Why are there cats on this set, anyway?" Jessica asked her.

"Quentin's trying to capture the look of ancient Rome. Apparently, the ruins are overrun with stray cats," Shelly explained.

"Well, it will certainly look authentic," Jessica said, placing the bowl on the floor. The five cats scrambled to get at the food.

"*Sss!*" hissed the biggest cat. Soon all of the cats were yowling and clawing at each other. Jessica quickly grabbed the bowl of food from the ground, and the cats all clambered around her, meowing loudly.

Quentin glared at them. "What is this, the set of *Cats*?" he burst out.

"Oh, boy," Jessica muttered under her breath. "Do we have any more bowls?"

Shelly handed her a stack of bowls, and Jessica lined them up on the table, quickly filling them up with food.

"Oww!" Quentin yelped suddenly. Jessica looked over and saw Quentin rubbing his thigh on the set. He had obviously walked into a fake boulder.

"Jessica, what's that rock doing in the middle of the floor?" Quentin yelled.

Jessica sighed. Quentin was definitely losing it. The rock was right where he had told her to put it five minutes ago. "I'll get it in just a sec," she said, pushing back a strand of dirty hair.

"Get it *now*," he barked out.

"Fine," Jessica responded angrily, placing all the bowls of food on the floor and heading to the set. She was just about at her wit's end. She had spent the last few hours pushing around piles of rocks, and now she had to push them back. Her arms were killing her from lifting the heavy boulders, and she was hot and dusty from building the framework of the acropolis.

Quentin's obviously forgotten about our date last night, Jessica thought as she eyed the huge gray rock. He was so stressed out about Simone that he had been screaming at Jessica for the past two hours. But Jessica had managed to keep her cool. She was hoping that Simone wouldn't show and that Quentin would use Jessica in her place.

Jessica picked up the boulder with both arms and staggered to the right, dropping the boulder on the edge of the set. A cloud of sawdust rose in the air and Jessica coughed, choking in the dust.

"I can-not be-lieve this," Quentin yelled, looking at his watch. "It's not possible." He charged from one end of the set to the other like a hungry lion. Then he sunk down into a low director's chair and dropped his head in his hands. "How am I going to get another model on such short notice?" he moaned.

Jessica took that as her cue. She didn't look much like model at the moment—covered from head to toe in particles of dust—but that couldn't be helped. Now was her chance, and she had to grab it.

Smoothing her hair down, Jessica headed in his direction. "Um, Quentin," she began. "If you'd like, I would be happy to—"

But just then Simone breezed in, looking

entirely unperturbed. "Good morning, everybody," she said cheerily. Despite her chipper tone, she looked exhausted. Her skin was pale and wan, and her eyes were sunken into her face. *Probably from dancing all night with my sister's boyfriend,* Jessica thought in disgust.

Quentin flew out of his chair at the sight of her. "Simone, do you know what time it is?" he demanded, practically purple with rage.

Simone looked at her watch. "Eleven o'clock," she responded sweetly.

Quentin shook his head. "I'm not even going to be able to develop this film myself. I'm going to have to FedEx it to New York at lunchtime, and they'll have to turn it around there."

Simone shrugged. "So?"

Quentin looked like he was about to explode. "*So?* So—you aren't the only model in this industry. Maybe you should think about that the next time you decide to show up two hours late!"

"Humph," Simone pouted, swiveling on a high heel and waltzing away. "I'll be in wardrobe."

As Jessica listened to the angry exchange, a brilliant idea popped into her head. Maybe she would get her chance to stand in for Simone after all. . . .

"Hello, Leona Peirson's office," Elizabeth said into the phone on Monday morning. She was sitting behind Leona's desk, up to her elbows in work. She was doing research for an article on life conditions of women in ancient Greece and fielding Leona's calls as well.

"Yes, this is Rupert Perry," said a deep male voice. "I'd like to set up a meeting with Leona for early next week."

"Uh, just one moment," Elizabeth said, frantically running a finger down the office directory for his name. Then she found it. Rupert Perry was the head of marketing.

Her screen beeped, indicating that her Library of Congress search was complete. "Five articles found," it read. "Continue searching?" it prompted. Elizabeth pressed "y."

"What day would be good for you, Mr. Perry?" she asked into the phone.

"Just a moment. I need to check my schedule," he responded.

There was a sharp knock on the door, and Anne, the receptionist, popped her head in. "Is the report for the meeting ready?" she mouthed.

Elizabeth nodded and held up an index finger. Cradling the phone on her shoulder, she clicked the mouse and switched windows on her computer screen. The editorial board was meeting to go over the report Leona had dictated to Elizabeth on Friday, and Elizabeth had typed it up. She scanned the screen and printed it out, handing it to the receptionist.

"Thank you," Anne said.

Elizabeth nodded, turning her attention back to her call.

"How is next Thursday at two o'clock?" Mr. Perry was asking.

Elizabeth flipped through Leona's desk calendar. "That's fine, Mr. Perry. I'll just pencil you in."

Just then, the other line buzzed. Elizabeth ran her fingers through her hair, feeling frazzled. She didn't know how Leona managed to juggle so many things at once.

"Hello, Leona Peirson's office," Elizabeth said.

"Hello, Leona Peirson," said a familiar female voice.

"Leona!" Elizabeth exclaimed. "I'm so glad you called. It's been total chaos here, and I had to make some executive decisions for you. I typed up our notes from Friday for the board meeting today—is that OK?"

"That's perfect," Leona reassured her. "That's exactly what I was going to ask you to do. It looks like you can do my job as well as I can."

Elizabeth laughed, feeling relieved. "Not quite. I think one day is about all I can handle." She swiveled Leona's armchair around and leaned back.

"Well, actually, Elizabeth, I've got some bad news for you," Leona said. "I broke my leg skiing."

"Oh, no!" Elizabeth exclaimed, sitting up straight. "How awful. Is it serious?"

"Well, not really," Leona responded. "But I'm in traction for the moment, and I won't be able to move for a few days."

"I'm really sorry," Elizabeth said sympathetically.

"Me too," Leona said. "I'm itching to get to work."

"Well, I'll be happy to help you in any way I can," Elizabeth offered.

"Great," Leona said. "Have you got a pen on you?"

Elizabeth grabbed a yellow legal pad and pen. "Shoot," she said.

"OK," Leona said. "I need you to sit in on the meeting today and present our report. Get everybody's input and make any corrections you think advisable, and then circulate a memo to the entire editorial department—and circulate a copy to the heads of the other departments as well. Then I need you to thoroughly research our three feature articles on the Library of Congress database and Lexis/Nexis. Do a complete printout and article summary. Make sure you proofread and fact check any stories that come in as well. . . ."

Elizabeth's eyes widened. This was enough work for an entire department, not one person. In fact, Leona wasn't asking her to assist her—she was asking her to *replace* her.

Five minutes later, Leona got to the end of her list. Elizabeth shook out her wrist, which was tired from all the writing, and stared at the page, wondering how in the world she could possibly accomplish everything on it.

"Did you get all that?" Leona asked.

"Yeah, I think so," Elizabeth said slowly.

"Don't worry, Elizabeth, I've got the greatest confidence in you," Leona said.

"Thanks, Leona," Elizabeth replied, swallowing hard. She just hoped she wouldn't disappoint her.

"Oh, and can you take care of a few personal things as well for me?"

Elizabeth stared at the phone in consternation. This was going too far. "What did you have in mind?" she asked cautiously.

"Just a few errands, but make sure you make a note of them," Leona said, speaking quickly. "I need you to water my plants, pick up my calls, open my mail, respond to any invitations by phone or mail, and feed the cats."

Elizabeth's mouth dropped open. She had expected Leona to ask her for a few personal things to take care of at *work*, like watering the drooping plant on her desk. After all, she was an *intern*, not a personal assistant. And besides, didn't Leona have any friends who could take care of her personal life for her?

"I keep an extra pair of house keys in the right drawer of my desk," Leona added. "You can use those."

Elizabeth opened her mouth to suggest that a friend stay at the house when Leona spoke up again. "Listen, the doctor's here. I've got to go. Cover for me at the office, OK?" she said. "Just say I'm working at home. I don't want anyone to know that I took off to go skiing."

"Uh—uh, sure," Elizabeth stuttered.

"Thanks, Elizabeth. You're the best," Leona

said. "Oh, and don't forget to pick up my dry cleaning. And you might want to vacuum as well while you're there. Bye, love!" Then she hung up.

Elizabeth dropped the receiver with a clatter. First her boyfriend dumped her for a supermodel, then the editorial board rejected her idea. Now she was picking up her boss's dry cleaning. Was there some kind of curse on her life? How much worse could things get?

"Jessica, get me some water," Simone ordered. "My skin is getting completely dehydrated under these bright lights." She was standing in front of the ruins dressed in an emerald green sheath. With her slanted eyeliner and gold eye shadow, her face had the same mysterious appearance as the cats around her. A number of extremely good-looking Italian male models were posing in the background.

"I think her brain is dehydrated," Jessica whispered to Shelly by the makeup table.

Shelly shook her head. "I think her brain is *fried*."

"Jessica, did you hear me?" Simone repeated in a shrill voice.

"I'm sorry, did you shriek?" Jessica responded. But then she stood up and walked out of the room before Simone had a chance to reply. Just last week Jessica had brought up an entire case of mineral water, but Simone had already gobbled it all up. *The skin is the key to beauty,* Simone was fond of repeating. *And water is the key to the skin.*

Jessica pressed the button at the elevator bank, glad to get away from the dynamic duo for a few minutes. Quentin had been shooting Simone for the last hour, and she had been whining and complaining nonstop. Quentin was getting testier and testier by the minute, a sure sign that the shots weren't going well.

Fifteen minutes later, Jessica returned, lugging another case of French mineral water in her arms, as well as a basket of vegetables and dried fruit. She dropped everything in the wardrobe room and stretched out her aching neck. Then she took out a bottle of water and filled up a plate with celery sticks.

When she returned to the main studio, Quentin was kneeling in front of the camera, and assistants were running around adjusting the lights for the next shot. Simone was pacing impatiently along the set.

"Here you are," Jessica said sweetly, handing her a bottle of water and a glass of ice. "And look," she said, holding up the plate of celery sticks, "a yummy treat as well!"

"Quentin, can't you do anything about the insolent interns?" Simone complained.

Quentin glanced around the camera. "Can't you do anything about your incessant whining?" he responded.

Jessica grinned, scoring her first victory for the day.

"Humph!" Simone pouted, setting the glass down on a rock and pouring the effervescent water into it. One of the cats leapt onto the rocks and stuck his head into the glass, sniffing at the contents.

"Oh, how disgusting!" Simone complained. She held the glass at arm's length and held it out to Jessica. "Replace this immediately."

"My pleasure," Jessica said, handing her another glass. She had brought out a double of everything, anticipating Simone's every request.

"Thank you," Simone said tightly, taking a delicate sip.

"Hey, Jess, can you give me a hand over here?" Shelly called from the makeup table.

"Sure," Jessica responded happily, hurrying over to join her. Shelly was in the process of making up Antonio, a striking male model with dark features and an aquiline nose.

"What can I do for you?" Jessica asked.

Shelly waved a hand in the air. "Oh, I just wanted to get you away from her highness."

"Shelly, you're the best," Jessica said gratefully. She took a seat on a stool and opened a jar of base, trying to look occupied.

"Shelly says you're the one who put together the set," Antonio said to Jessica with a smile. "And from the looks of you, that's obvious."

Jessica glanced down at her dust-covered body ruefully. "Yeah, by the time I get done every day, I

148

look like more like the ruins then the set."

"Well, your efforts have certainly paid off," Antonio complimented her. "You've really done a professional job."

"An-ton-io!" Shelly complained in exasperation. "One more word out of you and I'm going to paint your face instead of your lips."

"Sorry, Shelly," Antonio said docilely.

"Shh!" Shelly instructed. She looked carefully at his coloring, then chose a compact. "Now close your eyes," she directed, covering his face with beige powder.

Suddenly Jessica heard a yowl and looked over at the set. One of the cats had ducked behind Simone's rock and another was circling the boulder. Suddenly the bigger can pounced on the smaller one. Soon the two cats were snarling and hissing.

"Uh-oh," Jessica said to Shelly. "I think Simone's getting caught in another cat fight. I better go break it up."

"Would somebody please control these felines?" Simone snarled.

Jessica jumped and hurried over to the refreshment table to distract the cats. She grabbed a box of dry cat food from the counter and knelt down, shaking the box hard. All of the cats came scampering over.

Quentin clapped his hands together. "OK, everybody take their places," he called. "The shot's ready." Quentin peeked into the lens of his camera, then stood up. "Simone, I want you front and center. Antonio, Marco, and Stefan, spread out and lean against the acropolis. Nice. Good. Simone, I want you sulky. Male models, you're expressionless. Jessica, get the cats on the set." Jessica quickly jumped up and hid behind one of the borders on the set, throwing pieces of food onto the floor. The cats quickly ran between the boulders, adding a mysterious feel to the setting.

"Great! Perfect!" Quentin breathed, taking the shot. Then he adjusted the lens and clicked the camera a few more times. "Thanks guys, that's it for you," he told the models.

The guys headed for wardrobe, and Simone followed quickly behind. "Wait, Simone, I'm not done with you," Quentin ordered.

Simone gave him an exasperated look and returned to the set. "I want some close-ups of you," he said, picking up the camera hanging around his neck. Kneeling down, he zoomed in with the telephoto lens. "Give me expression. I want passion, anger, frustration."

Simone stared blankly into the camera.

"*Expression*, Simone," Quentin repeated.

"Arggh," Simone grumbled, shooting him an annoyed look.

"Great!" Quentin said, taking the shot.

Simone put her hands on her hips and pouted.

"Nice!" Quentin yelled, clicking the camera again.

"I have had enough of this!" Simone declared, her eyes shooting sparks.

"Perfect!" Quentin breathed, moving in close to her and taking shot after shot.

Simone crossed her hands over her chest, her face was practically purple with rage.

Quentin stood up and rewound the film. "That's a wrap," he said.

"I am going directly to a spa at a location I have no intention of disclosing," Simone announced. "No one should even *try* to track me down, since I will be totally out of reach." Then she stomped out.

Jessica's ears perked up at Simone's words. With Simone out of the way, she might finally get a shot at modeling herself.

Quentin sunk into a chair. "Well, I'm glad I got at least one good roll of film. For the first several rolls, Simone looked so tired that I thought I was going to have to pour chicken noodle soup over her head."

What a great idea! Jessica thought.

"If anyone needs me, I'm in the darkroom," Quentin said, standing up.

Jessica watched Quentin walk away, and a devious idea popped into her head. She waited until he had disappeared into the darkroom, then she looked around surreptitiously. Everybody was engaged in an activity—the assistants were taking down lights, Shelly was packing up her tray, and the set designer was gathering the cats together.

Her heart pounding in her chest, Jessica walked

nonchalantly toward the camera. Then she clicked open the back of it, exposing the film. Holding her breath, she quickly shut it again. She glanced around the room quickly and let out her breath in a rush. Nobody had even noticed.

Jessica rubbed her hands together, unable to believe her luck. If everything went according to plan, she was on her way to stardom.

Todd screeched into the parking lot of the Mode building and jumped out of his black BMW. He knew Simone had a photo shoot this morning, and he was hoping to catch her before she left for the day.

He hurried through the revolving doors when he caught side of a tall, slim figure stalking out the opposite entrance. It was Simone, and she looked like she was in a hurry. She was still dressed in her modeling attire—a long, shimmering green dress—and she wore a determined look on her face.

"Simone!" Todd called, running after her.

Simone stopped, an annoyed expression on her perfect features.

Todd jogged up to her, his heart thumping nervously against his rib cage. Even though he had spent every evening with her this weekend, her presence still intimidated her. Especially when she was wearing four-inch heels that made her taller than he was—and when she had the blasé look on her face that she had on now.

"Oh, hi, Todd," Simone said when her reached her.

"Hi," Todd said. "Listen, I—" He ran his fingers through his hair nervously, suddenly embarrassed at what he had to say.

"Yes?" Simone prompted him, tapping a high heel on the gravel.

Todd clenched his jaw and forged on ahead. "Well, my parents found out that I went out with you, and I'm in a lot of trouble at home."

Simone rolled her eyes. "This again!" she said, throwing up her arms. "Really, Todd, aren't you a bit *old* to be getting in trouble? Believe me, you'll never get anywhere at this pace. If you want to make it in this business, you've got to be independent. You've got to be your own man."

Todd swallowed hard, feeling more like six years old than sixteen. "I know," he said quickly. "I've tried to explain that to them, but they don't seem to understand. So, I wanted to know if you'd like to come to dinner tonight. You see, maybe if my parents meet you—" Todd blushed. "And see how wonderful you are—they'll be more understanding about the time we spend together."

Simone had been steadily tapping her heel on the ground as he spoke. Now she glanced at her watch. "I'm sorry, Todd, but I can't make it tonight. Maybe another time."

Todd felt a pang in his chest, feeling hurt by her casual words and disparaging tone, but he tried not to let it show. "Sure, no problem," he said in a nonchalant voice. "I'll call you tomorrow, then."

Simone shrugged. "Fine, whatever," she said.

Then she turned and strode away.

Todd just looked after her, feeling younger than ever.

Jessica crouched down in a corner in the main studio, filing negatives in a photo box. Quentin had been ranting and raving for the past half hour, and Jessica was trying to remain as inconspicuous as possible. He had discovered his film had been exposed after returning to the main studio and was yelling generally at everybody for incompetence. Fortunately, Quentin thought it was a fluke and didn't assume that somebody had tampered with his camera.

Jessica wasn't the only one laying low. The lighting assistants were pretending to be busy with some lights in the back, and the set workers were all sitting along the wall, whispering among themselves. Michael and Shelly were standing together at the makeup table, quietly putting away beauty supplies.

Quentin raked his fingers through his scruffy blond hair. "Now we can't get the shoot done," he shouted. "Do you know what this means?" He didn't wait for an answer. "This means the layout will be delayed. Which means the entire issue will be held up. Which means I'll lose my job. Which means my career is *ruined*."

The set designer clicked open the back door, and a couple of assistants followed him, carrying lights in their hands. Then Michael headed quietly to his salon. Shelly pushed open the door of wardrobe a few minutes later, a huge makeup case in her hand. Jessica hunched over her work, trying to concentrate on arranging the negatives.

When Jessica looked up, she swallowed hard. It looked like everybody had slowly managed to slip out of the room. Now it was just Quentin and Jessica. Quentin was slumped over a table, holding his head and moaning to himself.

Jessica gathered together her courage and stood up. Now was her chance, and she had to grab it. Jessica walked over to him and laid a comforting hand on his arm. "That's really tough," she said softly. "There's no way we'll will be able to get another model here in time."

"I know," Quentin said in despair. He stood up and began pacing around the room agitatedly. "There's got to be *something* we can do," he said.

"Well, if you'd like, *I* could fill in for Simone," Jessica suggested.

Quentin hesitated, and Jessica held her breath.

"All right," he said finally. "We'll give it a go. After all, we don't have a choice, do we?"

Jessica shook her head quickly.

"OK, go directly to hair and makeup," Quentin ordered. "We have no time to spare." Quentin opened the door of the side room and yelled. "Hey, you guys, bring those lights back in here! We've got another model on board."

Jessica hurried out of the room before Quentin could change his mind. As she slipped into Michael's hair salon, her heart began pounding in excitement. Her career was about to be launched!

Chapter 12

"Ninety-one, ninety-three, ninety-five. . ." Elizabeth said, reading the house numbers aloud as she drove slowly down Ocean Lane during her lunch break. "Ninety-*nine*. That's it." Elizabeth pulled the Jeep to a stop in front of Leona's condominium, pausing for a moment to admire the idyllic setting. The apartment complex was surrounded by beautiful cherry trees, and it was located only a mile from the ocean.

Elizabeth fitted the key in the lock on the second floor and pushed open the door. "Wow," she exclaimed, whistling under her breath at the sight that greeted her. The apartment was a huge airy space with light wood floors and high cathedral ceilings. If it weren't for the separate rooms, the condo's interior would have resembled a loft.

Elizabeth set down her bag on a small, round, wrought iron table, taking in the stylish decor of the living room. Two black leather couches were arranged perpendicularly in the middle of the room, with a big glass table in front of them. A blue art deco clock hung on the wall, and shell pink Tiffany lamps added a hint of color to the stark room. But most spectacular of all was the view. The far wall of the living room was made entirely of windows, and the foamy, blue-green Pacific Ocean sparkled in the distance.

The apartment is just like Leona, Elizabeth thought. *Sleek, modern, and fashionable.*

"*Mrrw!*" meowed a cat, prancing into the room. Soon two identical Persian cats were rubbing against her leg.

"Hey, you guys must be hungry, huh?" Elizabeth said, leaning down and stroking their fur.

Elizabeth hurried into the kitchen and rummaged through the cabinets, finally finding a stack of canned cat food. One of the cats leapt onto the counter and the other clawed at Elizabeth's leg impatiently, meowing incessantly. "OK, OK, just a minute," she berated them, lifting the cat off the counter and dropping him on the floor.

Elizabeth opened a can of food and divided it between the two bowls, and then she filled up another bowl with fresh water. She took a quick look in the refrigerator, wondering what Leona ate. *Evidently not much,* Elizabeth thought, staring at the empty fridge. All that was in the refrigerator was a bottle of diet Coke and a half-eaten grapefruit covered in aluminum foil. She shook her head. If a starvation diet was how Leona managed to keep so thin, then Elizabeth didn't think it was worth it.

Elizabeth caught sight of a big blue watering can on a high shelf and remembered the plants. She reached up for it and filled it with lukewarm water. Returning to the living room, she carefully watered the giant rubber plants in the corner. Then she headed back to the kitchen, pausing to pick up a frame from the bookshelf. It was a shot of Leona with a tall, dark guy. *Hmm,* Elizabeth thought. *That must be Sam.*

Elizabeth put her hands on her hips and surveyed the space. *Leona really has everything,* she thought in admiration. Independence, success, a cute boyfriend. . . . *Someday,* Elizabeth thought, *this is exactly what my life will be like.*

Driven by curiosity, Elizabeth explored the rest of the apartment. She peeked into the bathroom and found a clawfoot tub and a whirlpool. The bathroom was done in lime green, with painted Spanish tiles on the floor and an elegant pink marble sink against the wall.

Then she checked out the bedroom. Unlike the rest of the apartment, the bedroom was soft and romantic, with delicate ivory linens on the bed and long white curtains that swept the floor. Elizabeth pulled open the door to the walk-in closet and gasped. It looked like Leona had more clothes than Lila Fowler. Her suits were arranged by color, creating a rainbowlike row. And on the door hung pairs and pairs of shoes. Elizabeth flipped through the suits, fingering the rich materials and admiring the soft colors. She stopped as she came upon an exquisite ivory-colored suit with big round pearl buttons. Unlike most of Leona's ensembles, this one had a short-cropped jacket that was to be worn buttoned-up.

Elizabeth lifted out the suit, wondering how she would look in it. Did she dare? She looked around quickly, but only a fluffy cat was in sight, curled up contentedly at the base of the bed. Then Elizabeth shrugged. Why not? After all, if Elizabeth wanted to be just like Leona, then she had to *feel* like Leona. Trying on her clothes would only help Elizabeth to emulate her.

Elizabeth quickly pulled off her own skirt and jacket and slipped into the luxurious woven silk. Pulling on a pair of Leona's beige pumps, she stood in front of the full-length mirror. Elizabeth gasped at her reflection. She looked professional, yet stylish. She turned, admiring the sharp cut of the suit. No wonder people said clothes make the man—or the woman.

Pretending she was Leona, Elizabeth strode into the living room and took a seat on the leather couch. The cat padded after her, jumping up and kneading her lap with his paws. "Hello, kitty," she said in Leona's deep modulated voice. She picked up a note pad from the glass coffee table, and pressed the play button on the answering machine. "Leona, it's your sister, Terri . . ." came the first message.

"Your sister Terri," Elizabeth scrawled, running a finger through her hair like Leona did. Ten minutes later, she had gotten to the end of the messages. Elizabeth set the pad on the table and stood up graciously.

She paused in the middle of the floor, feeling regal in her elegant surroundings. "Now what?" she said to herself, placing an imagined French-manicured hand on her cheek. "Oh, yes, the mail." Elizabeth picked up the pile of letters she had brought in and carried them over to the sleek black desk in front of the window. Perching on the chair, Elizabeth crossed her legs and slit open the first one with a gold letter opener. "Now what's this?" she asked. "Ah, an invitation to a runway show. Hmm, I'll have to check my calendar." The rest of the mail contained personal letters and bills. Elizabeth left the letters on the desk and tucked the invitation into her bag. She would have to compose a response at work.

Elizabeth stood up and stretched in the sun, looking in wonder at the beautiful blue-green ocean right in the backyard. She was having so much fun she almost didn't want to take off the suit and go back to work. She walked through the living room, fingering knickknacks and looking at photos.

Then a tape recorder on the side table caught her eye. "Hmm, I wonder what that's for," Elizabeth said aloud. She sat down on the couch and picked it up, looking at it curiously. She was about to press "play," but then she stopped herself, feeling a twinge of guilt. It was one thing to try on Leona's suits, but it was another to invade her privacy.

Then Elizabeth shrugged the feeling away. Leona had no right to make Elizabeth her personal slave. If she was going to have to come here every single day to take care of Leona's life, she might as well learn all she could.

Elizabeth leaned back into the plush leather couch and pressed "play." Leona's deep voice came through, dictating letters. Elizabeth listened as Leona read a letter to Rupert Perry, the head of marketing. She yawned as Leona went through a long list of marketing possibilities for the Greek and Roman antiquity edition.

Oh well, I've heard all this before. Elizabeth picked up the tape recorder and searched for the stop button, but then she paused suddenly at Leona's next words. "Letter to Gordon Lewis," Leona was saying. Gordon Lewis was the hotshot new publisher of *Flair* who had brought the magazine to L.A. a few months ago. "Note to myself," Leona said. "This letter is not to go through Elizabeth."

Elizabeth's eyes widened at the mention of her name, and she listened closely, pacing the carpet

162

and holding the tape recorder in her hand. "Dear Gordon," Leona said in a crisp, clear voice. "As you suggested, I would like to formally submit the idea we discussed on the phone. It's actually quite simple and has the benefit of bringing *Flair* into the age of interactivity. I propose a column tentatively titled "Free Style," a one-page article written by a *Flair* reader with her ideas on fashion. The column would of course conform with the theme of the magazine, and submissions would be accepted, thus guaranteeing the high quality of writing that we depend on at *Flair*. I would be happy to discuss my idea at the next editorial board meeting. With best regards—Leona."

Elizabeth was stunned. She rewound the tape and played it back again. Then she fell back hard on the couch and clicked off the tape. Slowly, the significance hit her.

Leona had never pitched the idea at the meeting. In fact, she had stolen it from Elizabeth. And now she was taking full credit for it. Elizabeth couldn't believe what she'd just heard. She dropped her head back on the couch, staring up at the high ceiling. Leona had been her idol.

Elizabeth felt a knot twist slowly in her stomach. She felt entirely betrayed. And devastatingly disappointed.

Jessica walked carefully down the hall to the main studio after lunch, her hips thrust forward in an imitation of Simone's walk. She was wearing Simone's green dress and four-inch platform heels. The art director had frantically hemmed the dress and taken it in at the sides, and Shelly had made up her face in glamorous golden tones. Jessica's blue-green eyes were accentuated with shades of green eye shadow, and mauve blush with hints of gold brought out her cheekbones. Michael had twisted her hair into long, golden curls that bounced lightly around her face as she walked.

Jessica paused at the door of the photography studio, suddenly hit with the enormity of what was happening. She was actually about to be photographed by Quentin Berg for the hottest magazine in the fashion industry. She wasn't just fooling around with Lila on the beach with a camera. This was for real. She had entered the big league. Jessica's tongue turned dry, and a thousand butterflies began flitting around her subject. Was she crazy? She didn't know anything about modeling.

Jessica closed her hand around the doorknob and squeezed her eyes shut, forcing herself to take long, deep breaths. *One, two, three,* she counted slowly, trying to regain her composure. She felt exactly like she did when she was about to go onstage. She had the same tightening in her chest and the same queasiness in her stomach.

Get into the part, she told herself. When she was nervous before a show, she calmed her anxiety by losing herself in her role. Now she tried to assume the part of an ancient goddess. Closing her eyes, she pictured a dusty acropolis in ancient Rome. She was Athena, and she had descended from Mount Olympus to find the man with whom she had fallen in love. He had dark curly hair and piercing brown eyes. Even though he was just a mortal, he looked like a god.

Feeling calm at last, Jessica opened her eyes. She straightened her back and held her head high, walking serenely into the main studio. Assistants were frantically assembling bluish lights, and Quentin was hunched over the camera. But the action stopped when she walked in, and all eyes turned to her. Jessica sucked in her breath, feeling suddenly nervous again.

Quentin whistled when he saw her. "You— look—*fabulous!*" he exclaimed.

Shelly grinned from the make-up table, giving her a thumbs-up sign.

Jessica let out her breath in a rush.

Quentin stood up and looked at his watch. "We've only got time to redo the last roll," he told Jessica. "We're just taking shots of you."

Jessica nodded, her heart hammering in excitement.

Quentin frowned. "If we had the time, I would go through the basics of movement with you. Why don't you just walk around the set for a few minutes to get warmed up? I'm going to follow you with the lens and get the camera in focus."

Jessica nodded and walked onto the set, taking her place in front of the ruins. Moving gracefully, she threaded her way carefully amid the fake rocks, her back squared and her head held high. When she reached the end of the stage, she lifted her arms up in the air and stretched, trying to relax all the muscles in her body. Leaning down and grabbing onto the edge of a rock, she slowly stretched out her vertebrae one by one. Then she walked back in the other direction.

Suddenly she noticed the camera was clicking. She turned quickly toward Quentin, a long golden curl falling over her eye. *Click*, went the lens.

"Great!" Quentin exclaimed. Then he jumped onto the set. "I'm going to position you for the next shot."

Quentin moved Jessica to the center of the set directly in front of the ruins. Then he lifted her left arm in the air and set it at an awkward angle above her head. Jessica quickly shifted her weight, adjusting her arm to a more comfortable position.

Quentin sighed. "Jessica, don't move. You've got to do remain exactly as I put you. OK?"

"OK," Jessica said, grimacing. Quentin put both her arms in the air above her head and joined her hands together. Then he turned her face way back so her chin was jutting out. Quentin stepped back to get a better look. "Now cock your hip far to the right."

Jessica did as she was told. Quentin made a diamond with his fingers and looked through it. "Perfect!" he breathed.

Is he kidding? Jessica wondered, desperately trying to keep still. She felt like some sort of ridiculous contortionist.

"OK, Jessica, hold that pose," Quentin said, taking his place quickly behind the camera. He fiddled with the lens and took the shot.

Jessica quickly let her hands down and stretched out her neck. All her muscles ached already.

"Now we're going to take a few close-ups," Quentin explained. He knelt down and adjusted the telephoto lens. "Listen to me carefully," he directed. "You're in Rome, and it's hot. Think passion, sparks, fire."

Jessica closed her eyes and imagined the dusty smell of a hot, dry ruins. She jutted out a hip and stared sultrily into the camera.

"Great!" Quentin said, clicking the camera.

"OK, now put your right leg out and your hands on your hips. You're ancient royalty, a Roman empress."

Jessica gazed regally out at the camera, and Quentin took a number of shots.

Quentin paced a few feet, his eyes narrowed in thought. Then he nodded to himself and turned back to her. "Jessica, get in front of the acropolis," he directed. "Guys, I want rain!" he yelled out.

Rain! Jessica thought. She looked on worriedly

167

as Nick Nolan and the set assistants hastily constructed an artificial rain machine. One of the assistants set up a window fan on the floor, and another lugged buckets of water onto the set.

"Ready!" Nick called a few minutes later.

"OK, Jessica, let's have a smile," Quentin directed from behind the camera. "Guys, action!"

Jessica stared at the camera, a terrified smile frozen on her lips. Suddenly the fan turned on and drops of ice cold water sprayed over Jessica's body. Jessica gasped and recoiled instinctively.

"Jessica, don't react!" Quentin ordered. "Hold your head high and keep your body perfectly still. And keep gazing straight at me, right through the spray." Jessica stared at the camera and forced a shaky smile on her face, trying not to blink as cold drops of water cascaded over her head.

"OK, fan off," Quentin instructed quickly. The water stopped abruptly, and Jessica shivered, shaking out her hair and wrapping her arms around her body. "Shelly, we need wind," Quentin said.

Jessica looked on in horror as Shelly came onto the set with a huge hair dryer in her hand. The next thing she knew she was being blow-dried by the makeup artist.

"Nice," Quentin said, moving in close. "Jessica, look straight at the dryer and throw your head back." Jessica's hair flew back in the wind and a gust of warm air hit her cheeks. She trembled at the sudden change in temperature.

Finally Quentin took the last shot. "Thanks everybody! That's a wrap," he called out.

Jessica breathed a sigh of relief and collapsed onto a rock. Grabbing a towel, she wrapped it around her body, not sure if she was hot or cold. She shook her head ruefully. Modeling was more work than she had realized.

Jessica sailed into the mail room late that afternoon, a Federal Express package in her hand. She felt like she was walking on air. Even though the shoot had been difficult, it had gone without a hitch. With the talented photographer behind the camera, she was sure she was going to look great. Quentin had sent her down to the mail room right after she had changed. He wanted her to FedEx the negatives to New York to be developed.

Jessica stopped at the desk in the front room, surprised that Cameron wasn't working behind the counter. A lanky guy she didn't recognize was in his place, throwing boxes onto the loading dock.

The guy heard her approach the counter and turned around. He had longish red hair and watery blue eyes. "Can I help you?" he asked.

"Yes, I'm Quentin Berg's assistant," she said. "We need to FedEx this package to New York for an immediate turnaround." She handed the guy the Federal Express package. "It's extremely important," Jessica added.

169

The guy nodded. "Tell Mr. Berg not to worry. I'll take care of it myself."

"Thanks," Jessica said, turning around to go. Then she paused in thought. Since she was in the mail room, she might as well find Cameron. After all, today was clearly her day. She was sure Cameron would forgive her for her little twin switch.

"Do you know where Cameron Smith is working today?" Jessica asked. She hoped he wasn't off somewhere delivering a package in the building, because then she'd never be able to find him.

The guy's forehead creased in thought. "Today's Monday, right? He should be at the computer, keying in our weekend deliveries."

"The computer?" Jessica asked.

The guy nodded. "There's a computer alcove behind the shelves in the main room. You can't miss it."

"Thanks," Jessica said, hurrying around the counter. She walked through the dark halls of the cluttered mail room until she came to a set of standing wooden bookshelves. She looked around them. Sure enough, there was a small workspace set up, and Cameron was hunched behind the computer, peering at the screen.

Jessica's stomach fluttered at the sight of him. He was wearing a red plaid denim shirt and a blue baseball cap, with a few dark curls peeking out. He looked cuter than ever.

Cameron looked up as she walked in the doorway, scowling when he saw her.

But Jessica breezed in, undaunted. "Hi!" she said, flashing him one of her best smiles.

Cameron barely looked up from the keyboard. "Don't bother with the cover-girl charm, Jessica," Cameron said in disgust. "I'm not crazy about being yanked around like a puppet." Cameron scraped back his chair and stood up, ripping a long list out of the printer. "You may be able to get away with pulling stunts like that with other guys, but I'm not going to be anybody's second choice."

Jessica felt as though the floor had dropped out from under her. For a moment, she was speechless, surprised at how devastated she felt by Cameron's brush-off. Her good mood was totally gone. Suddenly the photo shoot didn't seem to matter at all.

Staring into his angry brown eyes, Jessica had a startling revelation—she was in love with Cameron Smith. And now that she'd gotten what she wanted from Quentin, there was nothing to stop her from going out with Cameron.

"Please, Cameron, just give me a chance," Jessica begged, tears coming into her blue-green eyes.

But Cameron wasn't moved. "A chance to what?" Cameron spat out. "To yank me around again?"

"A chance to explain," Jessica said softly.

Cameron crossed his arms across her chest. "Fine, say what you have to say."

171

Jessica took a deep breath, finding telling the truth a lot harder than inventing a story. "Well, I talked Elizabeth into doing a twin switch on Friday night because, because—" Jessica hesitated.

"Because?" Cameron repeated sharply.

"Because I had a date with Quentin as well," Jessica said in a rush. "And I didn't know how to get out of it."

Cameron's face darkened. "Mail-room guy not good enough for you, huh?" he spat out.

"No, that's not it at all," Jessica protested. "Cameron, I promise, that's—"

But Cameron held up a hand. "Look, Jessica, I think I've heard enough. You're a lovely girl, but unfortunately your beauty is only skin deep." He shook his head in disgust. "I'm sure you'll make a great model," he said bitterly. "You've certainly got what it takes."

And with that, he turned and stomped off.

Jessica stared after him, tears springing to her eyes. Now what was she going to do? She heard the back door open, and she jumped as it slammed shut.

Then Jessica turned and ran after him. Cameron was the one she really loved. Now she knew that for sure. She couldn't let him leave like this.

Jessica ran through the dark corridor, dodging packages, until she came upon a pair of big red double doors. Swinging through them, Jessica found herself in the back lot of the Mode building. She blinked in the sunlight, looking around for Cameron. Then she saw him, sitting on a bench. *Their* bench—the bench where they had shared their first lunch together.

Jessica approached him slowly. "I didn't realize you were eating at Chez Bench today," she said. "Is there room enough for two at your table?"

Cameron didn't crack a smile.

"All right," Jessica said, walking in a small circle in front of him. "You don't have to say anything. Just listen, OK?"

Jessica drew a haggard breath, summoning up her courage. "You see, Quentin asked me out before you did, and I didn't think I could break it off with him." She kicked at the gravel. "He is my boss, after all, and I guess I wanted to get a chance at modeling." Jessica looked down. "I know that's not a good reason, but that's the only reason. I promise."

Jessica paused for breath. "And I didn't think you'd understand," she finished softly. Jessica sat down on the bench, looking deep into his eyes. "I know now for sure that I'm not interested in Quentin. And I promise that from now on you'll be the only guy for me." Jessica looked down at the ground. "That is, if it's not too late."

Cameron frowned. "I've got to think about it, OK?"

Jessica swallowed hard and nodded, trying to hold back her tears. "OK," she whispered.

She stood up to walk away, but suddenly Cameron grabbed her and pulled her back onto the bench. Then he wrapped his arms around her and brought his lips to hers, kissing her so passionately that Jessica's breath was swept away. Jessica closed her eyes and kissed him back with all of her pent-up emotion, feeling shocks of sparks spread through her entire body.

"I've thought about it," Cameron said, laughing as they pulled back. "And I've decided to give you one more chance. On one condition."

"Anything," Jessica said breathlessly.

"That you go out with me tomorrow night," Cameron said.

Jessica happily agreed. "OK, but this time it's my treat. And we're having burgers and fries."

"What? No frog legs?" Cameron asked with a grin.

Jessica shook her head vehemently.

"But just one more thing," Cameron said, waggling a finger at her. "Tomorrow night, I don't want to go out with any split personalities. You got that?"

"Got it," Jessica said happily.

Enid rushed into her house after work, flying high from her internship at Morgan Agency. They were shorthanded at the literary agency today, so she got to do some real editorial work—which meant talking to a few authors directly and proofreading a manuscript. It had been thrilling to be so involved in making a book. Plus, she had made a suggestion to the literary agent about editorial changes to an autobiography, and the editor had loved the idea.

Enid took the steps upstairs two at a time and ran into her bedroom, throwing her backpack on the floor and flopping down on her bed. She flipped on her side and picked up the phone, instinctively punching in Elizabeth's number. As the phone rang, Enid waited in anticipation, excited to share her news. But then she heard the phone pick up and she hung up quickly. She had forgotten. Elizabeth wasn't her friend anymore.

Enid stood up and kicked at a T-shirt on the blue carpet. She caught it in her hand, and threw it on the bed. Then she slumped down in a chair, feeling a gnawing sense of emptiness inside of her. Her life wasn't the same without Elizabeth in it.

Feeling restless, she picked up the phone again and dialed Maria's number.

Maria answered on the first ring.

"Hey, it's Enid," Enid said. "Listen, have you heard anything from Elizabeth?"

"Not a word," Maria said. "Why, have you?"

"No, nothing," Enid said.

"Well, that's just as well," Maria said. "We can have more fun without her."

"That's true, I guess," Enid said slowly.

"Just look at what an awesome time we ended up having on our horrible date. We don't need

Elizabeth *or* dopey guys to have fun," Maria insisted.

"Right," Enid said softly.

"Right," Maria answered.

Enid hung up the phone slowly. She knew that she and Maria had fun on their date, but she couldn't seem to recall the feeling. And she knew Elizabeth had been a bad friend, but somehow she didn't feel angry anymore.

Enid walked slowly across the room, deep in thought. Enid and Elizabeth had been best friends for a long time. And that should count for something. After all, for Elizabeth to have a total personality transformation must mean that Elizabeth wasn't doing well.

Maybe Elizabeth's not the one being the bad friend, pondered Enid. *Maybe I am. Maybe she needs me now.*

Chapter 13

Tuesday morning, Elizabeth lay comatose in bed, staring at the ceiling. After her horrible discovery at Leona's yesterday, she had gone straight home. Then she had sat in front of the TV watching reruns for eight hours. What was left of her spirit was totally sunk. She decided she'd spend the rest of the week at home. In bed. She had no will left to go to work. Everything was meaningless.

Elizabeth had been awake since nine A.M., and she had been staring at the ceiling for three hours. She had now memorized every crack and every shadow.

Elizabeth's stomach growled, but the idea of food made her nauseated. And the concept of standing up and going all the way down the steps was unthinkable. In fact, she didn't feel like she'd ever have the energy to move again. She was utterly disillusioned.

Now she realized that everything she thought had value was all bogus. Work was bogus—having ideas and working hard didn't get you anywhere. All that counted was money and power. Relationships were bogus—being a loyal girlfriend and a good person didn't matter. All that mattered were long legs and fame.

Elizabeth followed the crack on the wall to the corner, feeling as though that's where she had ended up—in some corner at the end of a blank wall. Ethics and ideals didn't matter at all. People who followed their beliefs just ended up where she was—alone and a failure. Her life had no purpose.

The phone jangled loudly and Elizabeth didn't pick it up. It rang five times. Then the person called back. Elizabeth sighed, wishing that everybody would leave her in peace. Finally she reached out a lead-weight arm and brought the receiver to her ear.

"Yes," she said in a monotone voice.

"Elizabeth, it's Reggie," said a female voice.

"Hi, Reggie," Elizabeth responded flatly.

"Why aren't you at work?" Reggie asked, her voice full of concern. "Are you sick?"

"You could say that," Elizabeth said, flopping over on her side and holding the phone to the ear. The position was uncomfortable and she sat up, twirling the phone cord around her fingers.

"What's wrong? Do you have a flu?" Reggie pressed.

"No, just have a small case of disillusionment," Elizabeth answered wryly. "I'm sure it'll get better in a few years."

"Uh-oh," Reggie said. "Did something happen with Todd and the Fashion Witch?"

Elizabeth sighed and stood up, cradling the phone in the nook of her shoulder. "I don't want to talk about it." She dragged the phone across the room and curled up in her refurbished velvet chaise longue chair in the corner.

"OK, I understand," Reggie said. "Then how about lunch? It will do you good to get out of the house. I don't know what's bothering you, but I know for sure that your bed is not going to help."

"No, thanks, Reggie, I don't have the energy," Elizabeth said, laying down flat on her back on the chaise longue. She studied the lines on the ceiling, noticing that the shadows were different from this angle.

"OK, then, I'll drive out to Sweet Valley and we'll go someplace near you," Reggie suggested.

Elizabeth's eyes widened. Why wouldn't Reggie accept no for an answer? "Listen, I appreciate the offer, but I have no appetite," Elizabeth said. And the idea of getting up and getting dressed seemed to demand an infinite amount of energy.

"Nope, I insist," Reggie said in a firm voice. "Café Felix in Sweet Valley at one o'clock."

"But —" Elizabeth protested, sitting up quickly.

"And if you're not there, I'm going to come over and drag you out of bed," Reggie warned. Then the line clicked off.

Elizabeth groaned and fell back in the chair.

"*Mmm,* this is *luscious,*" Maria said, taking a big bite out of the pizza she and Enid were sharing.

Enid and Maria were at Guido's Pizza Palace in Sweet Valley for lunch on Tuesday. Enid had called Maria that morning at work and asked her to meet her there to discuss something important: *Elizabeth.* After talking to Maria last night, Enid was convinced they were being bad friends. Something told her Elizabeth needed them now.

"Want a bite?" Maria asked, offering Enid her slice.

Enid shook her head, making a face. "Are you kidding? Pineapple and tomato? I think I'll stick to my side of the pizza—mushrooms and eggplant. It's a lot safer."

"C'mon, just try it," Maria urged.

Enid picked up the pizza cutter and cut off a tiny end of Maria's slice. Then she nibbled at it cautiously. The pineapple was sweet and juicy, and it brought out the flavor of the pizza.

"Hey, this is great!" Enid exclaimed. She took a whole slice and put it on her plate.

Maria laughed, taking a long draw on her lemonade. "See? What'd I tell you?"

Enid took a big bite of pizza. "*Mrmph mrmm mm mmrph.*"

"You can say that again," Maria said with a chuckle.

Enid swallowed and wiped off her mouth. "I said, I'll never doubt you again."

Enid lapsed into silence after that, unsure as to how to broach the topic. Maria seemed adamant about ignoring Elizabeth until she apologized for her behavior. Enid was worried that Maria would convince her that was the best way. Or that Maria would feel betrayed. After all, if Enid started talking to Elizabeth and Maria didn't, then that would put a serious wrench in Enid and Maria's friendship. The last thing Enid wanted was to have to choose between Maria and Elizabeth.

Finally Maria pushed away her plate. "So, you said you wanted to discuss something important?" she asked.

"Yeah, actually, I did," Enid said slowly. "It's about Elizabeth. I've been thinking about the situation a lot, and I think we should reconsider our position. After all, we've both been friends with Elizabeth forever. She's been one of your best friends since second grade, and she's been my best friend all through high school."

Enid stopped for air. She had been hesitant to speak, but now the words were coming out in a rush. "Elizabeth's always been a wonderful friend," she continued. "She's always been loyal, considerate,

181

and there for us. This is one of the first times she's actually let us down. And it's not really that big of a deal." Enid took a deep breath, but forged on ahead. "I think we should give her another chance," she finished. "I think she needs us now."

Enid looked at Maria nervously, worried that she would think she was abandoning her. But Maria was nodding her head. "I know," she said. "I completely agree with you. In fact, I was thinking the same thing."

Enid brightened. "You were?"

Maria nodded. "Yeah. Even though we've been having a wonderful time hanging out together, something isn't right. Something's—missing."

"Elizabeth," Enid supplied.

"Exactly," Maria confirmed. "I don't think either of us have totally honest with ourselves—or with each other."

Enid breathed a sigh of relief. "Boy, am I glad to hear you say that," she said. Then she leaned forward. "So it's agreed? We're going to give Elizabeth another chance?"

Maria smiled and nodded. "I think she's learned her lesson by now."

"Elizabeth, you showed up!" Reggie exclaimed happily as Elizabeth walked into Café Felix in downtown Sweet Valley. The tiny restaurant was packed, and Reggie was standing at the front of the line at the hostess's podium.

"Well, you didn't give me much of a choice," Elizabeth said, joining her in line. Actually, she was glad Reggie had dragged her out of bed. She felt better now that she'd showered and gotten up.

"You know, for someone who's in a state of depression, you look pretty good," Reggie said. Elizabeth was just wearing faded blue jeans and a pale yellow sweater, but she had washed her hair and put on some lipstick.

Elizabeth shrugged. "That's because I slept for about fifteen hours last night."

"Ms. Andrews?" the hostess asked.

"That's us," Reggie confirmed.

"Right this way," the hostess said, leading them to a small round table out on the terrace. The restaurant overlooked a quaint old street in Sweet Valley, and the calm blue ocean shimmered in the distance.

"The office has erupted into chaos without you and Leona," Reggie said as they sat down.

"Oh no! What do you mean?" Elizabeth asked in alarm.

"Well, I guess Leona's been getting a million calls about the report that you typed up yesterday— you know, suggestions and stuff. And Anne's been pulling her hair out trying to field all the calls."

Elizabeth grimaced, but refused to let herself feel responsible. "Well, this time Leona's going to have to bail herself out of her own mess," she asserted.

Reggie gave her an odd look, but then the waiter appeared. "Are you ready to order?" he asked.

"Actually I'd just like a salad," Reggie said. "What do you have?"

"Chef's, *niçoise*, Caesar, Caesar chicken, goat cheese, and arugula," recited the waiter.

Reggie laughed. "I guess you get asked the question a lot," she said. "I'll just have the chef's salad."

"Me too," Elizabeth said. "And a glass of mineral water as well, please."

"Coming right up," the waiter said, picking up their menus and walking away.

Reggie looked at Elizabeth with curiosity. "So I guess all this has something to do with Leona?"

Elizabeth turned around to make sure the waiter was out of earshot. Then she leaned in across the table. "Listen, Reggie, this is strictly confidential. If I tell you the story, do you promise not to breath a word of it to anybody?"

Reggie nodded. "On my honor."

Elizabeth took a deep breath. "OK. Well, it all started last weekend when Leona took off work to go skiing in Lake Tahoe. She asked me to cover for her at work on Monday."

Reggie lifted an eyebrow. "I'm not surprised. That woman is complete devoid of ethics."

Elizabeth nodded, giving Reggie the whole story of Leona's betrayal—from Leona's broken leg to her request that Elizabeth take care of her personal life to the incriminating tape that Elizabeth had found in her house.

The waiter appeared and the girls quieted down as he set their salads in front of them.

"So that's the whole story," Elizabeth said when he'd left. "The upshot of it is that Leona stole my idea and is trying to take all the credit for it." Elizabeth picked up her fork and took a huge bite of salad, suddenly feeling her appetite return. She hadn't eaten anything since dinner the night before. Just sharing the story with Reggie had raised her spirits considerably.

Reggie shook her head in disgust. "I wouldn't have thought that even the dragon lady would do such a despicable thing." Reggie had been negative about Leona ever since she had met her, and now Elizabeth could see why.

Reggie's eyes narrowed in thought. "Do you have any proof that the idea is yours?" She buttered a piece of warm French bread and took a bite.

Elizabeth pondered that one. "Well, I did write up a lot of notes," she said, but then her face fell— "and gave them all to Leona." Elizabeth shook her head sadly, spreading out her hands in a wide gesture. "Reggie, it's hopeless. I don't have any proof at all."

"Wait, don't give up so fast," Reggie countered. "We don't even know if she's sent out the letter yet. Who did she address it to?" Reggie took a last bite of her salad and mopped up the dressing with a piece of bread.

"Gordon Lewis," Elizabeth said.

Reggie whistled under her breath. "Gordon Lewis!" she exclaimed. "Leona sure goes right to the top, doesn't she?"

The waiter picked up their plates, and Reggie ordered two coffees.

Elizabeth drummed her fingers on the table, deep in thought. "I wonder if there's any way we could schedule a meeting with him," she said.

"Well, you know I'm all for that," Reggie said with a grin. "I'd give anything to meet him—and to put Leona in her place."

Reggie had a wild crush on Gordon Lewis, and Elizabeth had no trouble understanding why. The girls had caught sight of him one day at the Mission Café in L.A., and Elizabeth had to agree with Reggie that he was one of the handsomest men she had ever seen. He was tall and distinguished-looking, with longish brown hair, bright blue eyes, and chiseled features.

The waiter set down their coffees in front of them, and Elizabeth poured a sugar packet into hers. She stirred it slowly, her mind clicking as she tried to think of a way to catch Leona in her own trap. She took a sip of coffee, and suddenly it hit her. Elizabeth practically spit out her coffee.

"What happened? Did you just get hit with inspiration?" Reggie asked.

Elizabeth nodded and grinned an evil grin. "Reggie, let me ask you something. How far would you be willing to go to accomplish both of your goals?"

Reggie's dark brown eyes glinted. "I'd go all the way."

"That's great!" Elizabeth breathed. She felt as though a huge burden had been lifted off her shoulders. Suddenly she had all her energy back. It wasn't true that ethics never won out. Sometimes you had to fight for them, that was all.

Elizabeth hunched over the table and spoke in a whisper. "If the two of us work together, we can teach Leona a lesson she'll never forget. We'll put the plan into action ourselves. And you just might get your shot with Gordon."

"I'm in," Reggie said with a smile.

"But remember," Elizabeth said. "This is top secret."

"Highly confidential," Reggie agreed solemnly.

They shook hands on the deal.

Tuesday night, Todd pulled into the driveway of his house in a foul mood. After Simone had blown him off that afternoon, he had decided he was sick of being pushed around. So he decided to find her. After all, Simone clearly appreciated aggressive, masculine men. Todd wasn't going to sit around any longer and let her call all the shots.

But he couldn't find her anywhere. He had

gone to all her favorite spots, but she wasn't anywhere to be seen. Then he had done the circuit of all the dance clubs they had frequented, but most of them were closed. Finally, he had driven to her apartment. Only Celia, her roommate, had answered the door, and she had told him abruptly that she didn't know where Simone was. But she did mention—before she shut the door in Todd's face—that Simone had left that afternoon with two full suitcases. Todd scowled. He couldn't believe she left town without telling him.

Todd sighed as he pushed open the front door, expecting an explosion. His mother had made a special dinner tonight, and he had promised he'd be there for it. He had meant to call home to say he would be late for dinner, but he had gotten so caught up in his search that he had forgotten all about it. Now he was going to have to endure another lecture from his parents.

"Hello, Todd," his father said as he walked in. He had a serious look on his face.

"Hi, Dad," Todd responded tentatively.

"Why don't you take your coat off?" Mr. Wilkins said with a sigh. "I think we have to talk."

Todd gulped as he took off his jacket and followed Mr. Wilkins into the kitchen. His dad didn't sound mad—he sounded resigned. That was a bad sign. A very bad sign.

Mr. Wilkins sat down in a chair, and Todd took a seat opposite him, slinging his coat over the back of it.

Mrs. Wilkins brought a coffee pot to the table and joined them. "Did you have a nice evening, Todd?" she asked.

Todd swallowed, feeling guilty. "I'm really sorry about dinner, Mom. I meant to call." Todd raised his shoulders. "I guess I just lost track of the time."

Todd's mother patted his hand. "That's all right, dear," she said.

Now Todd was really worried. His mother wasn't angry either. Something ominous was definitely brewing in the air.

Mr. Wilkins poured some coffee into his mug and took a sip. "Well, Todd, you're obviously not concerned about following the rules of the household," he said. "When you didn't show up for dinner tonight, we were worried sick."

Mrs. Wilkins nodded. "We didn't know what had happened to you. We called Aaron and Winston and Bruce, but nobody knew where you were."

Todd could feel the heat rising in his body. He couldn't believe his parents had called all his friends. They were acting like he was in third grade. He was glad they didn't have school tomorrow, because his friends would be sure to tease him about it mercilessly.

"Even Elizabeth had no idea what you were doing tonight," his mother added.

At that, Todd practically exploded. His parents *knew* he and Elizabeth had broken up, and they knew he was going out with Simone. How could they call her? Didn't they have any tact? Did they want to rub the fact of their breakup in Elizabeth's face? Todd twisted his fingers together in his lap, forcing himself to remain quiet. He was obviously in enough trouble as it was.

"So, your mother and I have had a talk," his father said.

Here it comes, Todd thought, bracing himself for the worst.

"Todd, we've given you all our support with this modeling thing," his father began. "We agreed to let you quit Varitronics and take a shot at modeling, but clearly it's turning your head around." His father sighed. "We've tried everything we can. We tried grounding you, we tried scolding you. . . ."

Todd stared at his parents in horror. "What are you getting at?" he interrupted.

"Todd, I'm afraid you're going to have to give up modeling," Mrs. Wilkins said softly.

"What?" Todd protested. "No way. That's— that's ridiculous! Modeling doesn't have anything to do with this."

"Oh yes it does," his father replied. "Modeling has *everything* to do with it. Before, you were a normal teenage kid. Now you think you're some kind of superstar who can make his own rules."

Todd stared at his parents in shock. He couldn't believe they would dictate his life—and his career—like this.

Todd scraped his chair back and stood up, over-whelmed by shock and hurt. And in the background Simone's words echoed in his head. *Are you a man or a mouse, Todd? Are you a man or a mouse?*

I'm a man, Todd decided.

Todd folded his arms across his chest. "Well, I refuse to give modeling up," he said calmly. "You can't force me."

His father's voice turned stern. "Todd Wilkins, as long as you live under our roof, you're going to have to abide by our rules—and that means giving up your modeling career."

Todd faced his parents calmly. "Fine," he responded. "Then I won't live under your roof." He grabbed his jacket from the chair and shrugged it on. "I'll move out."

Chapter 14

Wednesday morning, Jessica arrived at work early, hoping to catch Quentin alone. He was supposed to have met with the editorial board late yesterday afternoon to go over their photo shoot, and Jessica was anxious to get the results. In fact, she was so nervous that she had barely slept at all the night before. When she finally did fall asleep, she just relived the shoot in her dreams. She felt like she had never left the Mode building.

As Jessica rode the elevator up to the eleventh floor, her heart pounded in anticipation. Even though Jessica was sure the shots would be fabulous, she was still nervous. After all, she wasn't quite tall enough to be a model. Plus, she was just an intern. She didn't know if the magazine would accept using her as a model. Not to mention that Elizabeth appeared to be on some kind of work

192

strike, which wasn't going to help matters.

When Jessica walked into the photography studio, it was entirely deserted. She flicked on the lights and walked around the room, looking for some kind of sign—the photographs or a report or a note or something. But she didn't come upon anything out of the ordinary—just the usual jumble of cameras and costumes and props.

Jessica's stomach fluttered nervously. This was it—the big moment. It was all or nothing. With Simone safely on vacation, now was her chance to make it as a model. If they liked her, they could use her for another shoot. But if they didn't like her . . .

Banish the thought, Jessica commanded herself. *Think positive.* She paced around the room, her imagination soaring. She pictured herself on the cover of *Flair* in her emerald green dress, her blue-green eyes dazzling as they stared at the camera. Then she saw herself in quick succession on the cover of every other big fashion magazine—*Ingenue, Fashion Forward, Bella.* . . . Jessica Wakefield would be plastered all over the newsstands—the newest and hottest supermodel ever. She envisioned important parties, gallery openings, runway shows . . . and everywhere she went, Cameron would be at her side, driving all her fans wild with jealousy.

Quentin walked into the room. "Ah, just the face I was hoping to see," he said.

Jessica popped out of her reverie and her mouth turned dry. She turned to face Quentin, but found that she had lost her powers of speech.

"Well, I've got good news for you," Quentin said. "The magazine loved your photos. If I want, I can use you for another shoot."

Jessica felt the blood rush to her ears, and she felt faint. Was it possible? Was she actually going to be featured in *Flair* magazine? It really was a dream come true.

But she played it cool with Quentin. "Naturally, you'll want to," she said coyly.

"I think I might need some convincing," Quentin said in a low voice. He grabbed Jessica in his arms and pressed his lips to hers, kissing her passionately.

"*Mmph!*" Jessica protested, placing her hands square on his chest to push him away. But then she heard someone clear his throat from behind them.

She turned around quickly and gasped. It was Cameron, and he was staring at her, his face a mask of stone.

Then he turned around and walked out without a word.

Jessica chased after Cameron, leaving a baffled-looking Quentin behind.

Panting, she caught up with him at the elevator.

"It's over, Jessica," Cameron said, his brown

eyes devoid of expression. "No more chances." Cameron stepped smoothly into the elevator.

"Cameron, wait—"

But the door of the elevator closed, and Cameron was gone.

Hot tears slid down Jessica's cheeks. *What have I done?*

Elizabeth sat in front of her computer at home, aggressively clicking away at the keys. She was composing a letter to Gordon Lewis, and she was creating a masterpiece. Elizabeth skimmed over what she had written, smiling in satisfaction.

Then she leaned back and went over the steps of her and Reggie's plan in her mind. Switching screens with her mouse, she quickly outlined the plan on the computer. Then she read through the scheme. *It's perfect,* she breathed. Their strategy was foolproof. It was simple, but effective—and sure to expose Leona Peirson for the fraud that she was.

Elizabeth drummed her fingers on her desk, anxious to put their plan into motion. For the first time in days, she was brimming with energy. She was sick of lying around feeling sorry for herself. She was ready to take action.

It's not true that ideals don't count, Elizabeth thought. But sometimes you had to fight for them. And fight she would. It was time to march into battle.

As she thought for the millionth time about Leona's deception, Elizabeth's blood began to boil. She picked up a pencil from her desk and snapped it in her hand.

Elizabeth's eyes narrowed. *I'm going to get revenge on the woman who betrayed me,* she vowed silently. *If it's the last thing I do. . . .*

Will Elizabeth's plan for revenge work perfectly—or lead her into danger worse than she ever imagined? Will Jessica manage to convince Cameron that they're meant for each other? And how is Todd going to survive on his own? Find out in Sweet Valley High #131, **FASHION VICTIM,** *the third and final book in this very fashionable three-part miniseries. Don't miss it!*

SIGN UP FOR THE SWEET VALLEY HIGH® FAN CLUB!

Hey, girls! Get all the gossip on Sweet Valley High's® most popular teenagers when you join our fantastic Fan Club! As a member, you'll get all of this really cool stuff:

- Membership Card with your own personal Fan Club ID number
- A Sweet Valley High® Secret Treasure Box
- Sweet Valley High® Stationery
- Official Fan Club Pencil (for secret note writing!)
- Three Bookmarks
- A "Members Only" Door Hanger
- Two Skeins of J. & P. Coats® Embroidery Floss with flower barrette instruction leaflet
- Two editions of *The Oracle* newsletter
- Plus exclusive Sweet Valley High® product offers, special savings, contests, and much more!

Be the first to find out what Jessica & Elizabeth Wakefield are up to by joining the Sweet Valley High® Fan Club for the one-year membership fee of only $6.25 each for U.S. residents, $8.25 for Canadian residents (U.S. currency). Includes shipping & handling.

Send a check or money order (do not send cash) made payable to "Sweet Valley High® Fan Club" along with this form to:

SWEET VALLEY HIGH® FAN CLUB, BOX 3919-B, SCHAUMBURG, IL 60168-3919

NAME _____
(Please print clearly)

ADDRESS _____

CITY_____ STATE _____ ZIP_____
(Required)

AGE _____ BIRTHDAY_____ / _____ / _____

Offer good while supplies last. Allow 6-8 weeks after check clearance for delivery. Addresses without ZIP codes cannot be honored. Offer good in USA & Canada only. Void where prohibited by law.
©1993 by Francine Pascal   LCI-1383-193